the cabbage garden

Fabiana Addy

Copyright © 2019 by Fabiana Addy
The right of Fabiana Addy to be
identified as the author of this work
has been asserted in accordance with
the Copyright, Designs and Patents Act 1988.
All rights reserved.

This is a work of fiction. Names, characters, places,
and incidents are either the product of
the author's imagination or are used fictitiously.
Any resemblance to actual persons,
living or dead, businesses, companies, events,
or locales is entirely coincidental.

Foreword

I've heard many people speak of books that changed their lives but, and it's only my opinion, no book has ever been written that did such a thing. They can offer guidance and advice or even clues as to what could change your life but that is all it is because there's only one thing that can change your life...you. Consequently, this book will not change your life.

As an author myself, I know the difficulty of words and their usage but there's poetry here in the language and descriptions used, the prose carrying one along from chapter to chapter with echoes of 'Through the Looking Glass'; an eccentric setting, a series of quirky characters and a quest.

Not all is as it seems. Is the door hidden in plain sight a reality or a sudden desire; could four simple words reveal it one way or another?

Dan Wheatcroft

To Paul,
my love and best friend.
Thank you for every day.

CONTENTS

Prologue
1. The mystery of Lavender Street
2. Lilac tree and cabbages
3. The art of entertaining
4. A peculiar and knowledgeable postman
5. It sounds exotic
6. Nonsense
7. Before we were interrupted
8. Not even close
9. Good advice, in all
10. Moderation and creativity
11. Multiple choices
12. Vandalism
13. That takes the biscuit
14. The scribe's daughter
15. The strawberry picker
16. False friends
17. Patience
18. Child's play
19. The wish
20. Oranges, bananas and unicorns

21. Nine stones
22. Murky waters
23. The right one
24. A mysterious little sheep
25. The answer is always nine
26. I don't like strawberries
27. Everything makes sense
28. The flower calendar
29. Then that's what I shall call you
30. Forty-five
31. It's not my cat
32. I travel light
33. Reality bites
34. Everyone has a key
35. An astonishing find
36. In and out of the woods
37. By some miracle
38. Snow in June
39. Gibberish
40. Freedom
41. The interview
42. Unexpected rescue

43. Pointless
44. The wrath of the goddess
45. A love song
46. The veil is lifted
47. On top of the world
48. Home
    Epilogue
    Afterword

"Stop prevaricating. You're looking in all the wrong places. Just listen to your heart. Start with simple, familiar things."

PROLOGUE

In a great city there once lived an old scribe whose family came from a distant land.

He ran his business in the central square, recording receipts and inventories, assisting various commercial transactions, settling disputes, and writing the occasional letter for the illiterate customer. Every now and again some high official would come for him and the old scribe would disappear for weeks on end. Nobody knew where or why.

In a land where few could read or write, scribal services were in great demand. Work was always abundant, and with work came money and status. Nonetheless, the scribe lived a simple and private life, devoting every spare moment to the one person he held most dear in the whole world, the only family he had left – his young daughter.

When she was ready, he taught her all he knew. They came from a long line of master scribes and that's how they passed on the secrets of their art from one generation to the next, over the millennia.

At first, the man tested his daughter's natural skills. Before she could talk, he gathered a few things and playfully placed them all in front of her – an array of mysterious toys to choose from. Among them, there was a clay tablet, a bowl of mouth-watering fruits, an eye-catching necklace, a small, artfully carved horse, a pile of sparkling silver, and a plain reed stylus. Without hesitation, his daughter picked up the stylus and, pressing it onto the clay tablet, started humming a song. Her choice would've been enough to prove she had the calling. It was the tune that intrigued her father. Out of curiosity, the man looked at the clay tablet, expecting to see just some childish doodling. When he saw the clearly drawn sign, the air rushed from his lungs.

1

THE MYSTERY OF LAVENDER STREET

The secret door, hidden in plain sight, now stood wide open, waiting for her to step through. But she simply couldn't get that little sheep out of her mind. And then there was the mystery of Lavender Street – this small block of flats, probably the oldest in Chesternutville, with its huge, seemingly endless cabbage garden.

"There must have been a lavender field around here," she once mused out loud.

Five other tenants happened to hear what she said, and they all quickly shook their heads. "No, we've never seen any lavender in this town. Perhaps it's just not the right climate for it."

It was. She knew it, but didn't insist any further. To them, she was just the girl who'd recently moved into a flat on the second floor, and she didn't want to upset them with unnecessary questions. They obviously loved their cabbage. Four days out of seven, the whole place smelled like cabbage heaven. And that was fine by her.

She'd come here for a reason, which had probably little to do with lavender, cabbage or climate zones. Now only to remember what the reason was. Along with everything else.

That night, in a dream, the girl saw the true lay of the land. Where the small estate building with its gigantic cabbage garden now stood, there was a long country road, with a dark wood looming on the left, and a meadow of waving grass, sprinkled with wildflowers, on the right. She was standing in the middle of the road, wondering how dangerous it would be to step onto that open field. In this reality that would make her an easy target.

When she woke up, the girl knew what she had to do. In her pyjamas, braving the dark of dawn, she sneaked into the communal garden and picked a row of cabbages. Then she put on a nice dress and went to sell them at the market.

The vendors from the other stands eyed her suspiciously. Who puts on a nice dress to sell cabbages?

The market was a hustle and bustle of determined housewives elbowing their way to the coveted fruit and veg stalls, and bargaining, like stormy birds of prey, with gruff, unyielding sellers. The girl from Lavender Street sold her cabbages quickly and, after she gave the last few away, she used the proceeds to buy some potted plants and a handful of seeds.

She was getting ready to leave when she spotted the boy in the distance. Apart from hers, his was the only smiling face in the whole marketplace. On a small stand, squeezed between two potato vendors, he was selling potted herbs that, from where she stood, looked like parsley, basil, thyme and... Lavender!

A shrill noise made her start. The girl turned her head for a second and when she looked back, the boy was gone – his small stall vanished into thin air. She rushed over and asked after him. All the vendors around shook their heads in disbelief. "Nobody sells herbs here. This has always been potatoes only."

Baffled, the girl returned to the cabbage garden and, in the row now laid bare, she planted red petunias, yellow marigolds and blue hardy geraniums interspersed with spinach and lettuce seeds, then went up to her flat to have a shower and feed the cat.

2
LILAC TREE AND CABBAGES

For the next seven days, every morning, she put on a nice dress and quietly slipped into the garden to water her row of flowers and seeds. Around her, cabbages would disappear here and there only for new ones to miraculously pop up in their place overnight. As hard as it was to overcome her shyness, the girl from the second floor faithfully tended her row of flowers and seeds day in, day out. The mere thought of being in the spotlight made her cringe, but she clenched her teeth and hurriedly carried on, though she didn't really understand what she was doing, and why the urge to do it at all. But it had to be done.

More often than not, she found herself thinking about the boy who had been selling potted herbs at the market and then suddenly disappeared. Something about his smile had silently spoken to her. It was a faraway bittersweet smile she somehow recognised. They could've been friends. He might've understood.

Friday night, she dreamt of flowers that contained mysterious numbers – a magical code which unlocked a secret message. The flowers released their colours into the wide open air, where they floated and danced like weightless balloons, higher and higher into the sky, releasing their fragrance which turned into music, and the music fell back towards the ground like a spring shower on a warm sunny day, embracing the world.

On Saturday, the block president called a tenants' meeting for five p.m. The girl from the second floor looked forward to getting to know everybody a bit better. In case her row of flowers was mentioned, she would tell them about companion planting, how certain flowers attract beneficial insects and repel pests. Surely her neighbours would welcome the idea.

At five p.m. sharp, the girl went to attend the meeting, but all she found was a notice on the front door, announcing in bold letters: '**The tenants' committee decided to have the lilac tree next to the building cut down.**' Underneath, in smaller print, was added: "Stealing cabbages is against the law and shall be sanctioned accordingly."

3
THE ART OF ENTERTAINING

Chesternutville was a triangle-shaped town that had everything: the sea on one side, the mountains on another and, for the locals' peace of mind, a great concrete wall running along its open border. The town dwellers felt sheltered, cosy and safe.

The following week was holiday week, so half of the tenants from Lavender Street went to the sea coast, and three quarters of the other half went to the mountains. On Monday, except for the block president and herself, the building was almost empty. Around three p.m. the girl decided to pay the man a visit and set things straight.

He opened the door in his striped pyjamas, block president jacket on top, and hurriedly ushered her into the living room. "May I offer you some coffee? Or maybe some tea. No, we've run out of tea... You see, it's usually my wife who takes care of these things, but now she's away on holiday. She went to the seaside."

"Don't bother, please. I just came to..."

"It's no bother at all. In fact, I insist!" And with that, before she could object, he disappeared into the kitchen.

The girl looked around, slowly taking in the mass of lace doilies covering every single surface in the room – the sofa, the coffee table, the chairs, the television set. The lady of the house, or the block president himself, must have been a crochet champion. One wall was lined with book shelves. However, the undisputed centrepiece of the room had to be the display cabinet on the adjacent wall, packed full with porcelain figurines. The top shelf sported ballerinas and dainty ladies in Victorian dresses, carrying the occasional amphora or flower arrangement, or just looking aloof riding a posh buggy. The mid-shelf had an obvious bohemian theme going – the drunkard poetically fallen in a wheelbarrow, two drunk pals leaning on each other, an intoxicated chap crumpled on a bench that looked about to give way. The bottom shelf, less dramatic, but just as random as the other two, hosted an improbable Zoo made of cute tiny puppies, geese, and other poultry, a huge tiger on the prowl, an even more imposing pair of pigeons, and a larger than life glass fish.

On the opposite wall, by the picture of Mr. and Mrs. Block President on their wedding day, hung a giant embroidered carpet that depicted a medieval looking man fleeing on horseback with a woman in his arms – presumably his beloved, or it might have been just someone he'd kidnapped; the nature of their relationship wasn't made altogether clear. They were being chased, or perhaps just followed, by a second horse rider whose intentions caused her uncertainty.

Right then the host reappeared, holding a tray with two steaming mugs and a packet of cigarettes. "Please, miss, take a seat," he said courteously, handing her one of the drinks and pointing to sofa.

The girl sat down and took a sip. It wasn't coffee; it was some hot fizzy drink that tasted like cardboard, but she didn't say anything. Actually, she did, but it was on a completely different matter. "You have an impressive collection."

"We've always been great art lovers, my wife and I," the host acquiesced with due poise, casting a proud look at the display cabinet. "See the drunkard sleeping on the bench? That's one rare piece, that, and hard to get too."

The girl didn't know exactly how to respond, so she just smiled politely and nodded her head.

"Of course, you're too young to own a piece of such value," he continued. "That's something one has to earn, through years of work, through sacrifice, through the relations one builds in a lifetime. It's all about knowing the right people in the right places. You see, I know this chap who works at the china factory…"

Feeling he'd given too much away, the block president stopped abruptly and changed the subject accordingly. "We are a non-smoking family."

"I don't smoke either."

"Nevertheless, we shall both light a cigarette." Before she could protest, he opened a book and read in a grave tone of voice: 'While only a few years ago smoking at the dinner table was considered inappropriate, nowadays cigarettes are served with coffee even in non-smoking households.' There you have it," he concluded with satisfied serenity, setting the book back on the table. "It's clearly stated in *The Little Guide to Entertaining Guests*."

They weren't sitting at the dinner table, and they weren't even drinking coffee, but the girl didn't want to be rude so she just went along. They both lit a cigarette and spent the next minute coughing.

"Anyway, I came to see you about that announcement," she began eventually, struggling to see him through the blue clouds of cigarette smoke.

"If it's on official business, we need a third party to witness our conversation." He opened the book again and read out loud: 'When making a guest list, the hosts must make sure to invite, among others, at least one or two conversationalists.'"

Fortunately that's when the doorbell rang. It was the postman, bringing the daily postcards sent from the mountains and the seaside by the holiday-makers.

"How's my wife doing?" the block president inquired.

"Great," the postman replied with a reassuring smile. "She sent greetings to Flat no. 8, along with a picture of herself enjoying a refreshing fruit cocktail on the sunny beach."

Since they were usually too busy with work and other various endeavours to spend much time interacting with their neighbours, the tenants from Lavender Street had come up with a brilliant system that helped them communicate without really having to do so: they sent postcards to one another, even when they weren't on holiday, and that's how everybody knew what everybody else was doing every night and every day.

Hence, while Mrs. Block President kept Flat no. 8 up to date with her activities, her husband now received word from the car mechanic living in Flat no. 12: the fresh mountain air had given him a sore throat, but the mulled wine and cough medicine were already working miracles. It was a random and cheerful system that worked wonderfully.

Of course, the most well informed people in town were the postmen, whose job was not only to deliver the mail, but to read it beforehand as well, just in case.

4
A PECULIAR AND KNOWLEDGEABLE POSTMAN

To become a Chesternutville postman one had to be nosy by nature. The postman appointed to Lavender Street was no exception, but he had a special gift. He could read between the lines.

"You're just the man we needed!" the block president exclaimed with a contented grin, inviting him in and then rushing off to fix another pot of fake coffee.

The postman sat down in front of the girl and smiled at her. "You are the young lady from the second floor who doesn't send or receive any postcards."

"I wouldn't know what to write," she smiled back. "My life is not all that exciting."

"How come you're not on holiday like everybody else?"

"I'm a freelancer," she said. "No fixed hours. In theory, I can work or take a break whenever I want."

The postman's gaze drifted towards the window. "The flowers you planted in the garden are lovely. It was high time someone did that. I just didn't expect it to be someone so young."

She started to say something, but just then the host returned with their drinks. "So, my good fellow," he good-naturedly addressed the postman, sticking to the etiquette of entertaining guests, "do you happen to have any hobbies?"

"As a matter of fact, I'm an aquarium fish aficionado," the postman replied with a promptness that took the girl by surprise. "They never cease to amaze me. There are species that can fly, one can walk on the bottom of the ocean, the white spotted pufferfish will create the most elaborate shapes in the sand, while the cave fish has no eyes and lives a peaceful and presumably fulfilled life without needing to see a thing."

"We had a goldfish once," the block president nodded knowingly. "But it died and we had to flush it down the toilet."

With that, feeling he'd said all that could be possibly said on the matter, the host pointed to the packet of cigarettes on the table. "Do you know any jokes?" he asked, coughing, while they were all smoking their mandatory cigarettes. The postman shrugged and shook his head.

"I'm not good at telling jokes, but I know a maths trick," the girl offered. Both men nodded in agreement, so she went on. "Think of a number – any one or two-digit number. Don't tell me what it is – just make sure you remember it. Now multiply it by 2. Done? Now add 18, divide the sum by 2 and subtract the number you thought of initially."

"I forgot what it was," moaned the block president.

"Not a problem. Do you still remember yours?" she asked the postman. He nodded. "Just choose another number," she added, glancing back at the host, "and this time make sure you remember it." The girl then slowly repeated the instructions.

"Wait, I need a calculator!" cried out the block president, jumping up and disappearing in the other room.

5
IT SOUNDS EXOTIC

The girl let her gaze drift over the crocheted artwork adorning the room. "I've always admired people who can do this – create beautiful things with their own two hands," she said thoughtfully, picking up her conversation with the postman where they'd left it. "I never could. Probably therefore the urge to plant something in the cabbage garden." She hesitated, but the postman's smile encouraged her on. "You see, my only skill is to translate things from one language into another. But that's so ... elusive. Now, all of a sudden, I feel the need to plant things in the solid ground and watch them grow – see them physically ... materially grow. And this way perhaps it will all eventually take shape and make sense."

Her eyes fell on the embroidered carpet, and she gave the postman a quizzical look.

"It's called *The Abduction From The Seraglio*," he explained, turning towards the embroidery hanging on the wall behind him. "At one time you would've found one displayed in almost every household in town."

"It sounds exotic."

"The scene was actually inspired by an opera composed in the late 1700s."

Having a better look the carpet, only then did she notice the small letters embroidered in the bottom left corner. *The sword won't fall upon a bowed head.* It was strange even to say that, let alone stick the words on a wall.

"This town has spent the best part of its history being invaded by greater powers," the postman began, answering her unspoken question. "They were almost always defeated, but never conquered. While the town was in fact controlled by one empire or another, the local rulers were given the impression they still had some control over their land and people. As illusionary as that autonomy might have been, the town dwellers found solace in it and that's how they came up with the saying 'The sword won't fall upon a bowed head.'"

"Cowardice?" she guessed. "Lack of self-esteem?"

"More like submissiveness used as a means of self-defence or self-preservation, as the case may be."

The girl slowly nodded. "I see ... It's not easy to stand up for yourself – hold your head up high."

"'To die, to sleep' _"

"Shakespeare." She smiled. "Have they made themselves heard since?"

"They are still keeping their voice down." The postman took *The Little Guide to Entertaining Guests* and thumbed through it. "This book was published a hundred years ago," he commented, then added benevolently: "You see, being stuck in the past can create some awkward situations."

The girl smiled a sigh. She was stuck too. Not so much in the past as in this indefinite moment that felt like a crossroads and at times like a dead end. She wanted to say something, but right then the block president burst back into the living room and declared in a flustered tone of voice: "I can't find the calculator! My wife is the one who usually takes care of these things – heaven knows where she's put it!"

"You could maybe pick another number," the girl suggested. "This time a 1 digit one so it's easier to remember and we could go through the steps one more time."

"A 1 digit number, you say? ... Let's see... No, that would make it way too easy for you!" huffed the host. "Oh, it's all so complicated! Why couldn't you just tell a joke? Or I could've told you a few good ones. Never mind. Let's just get it over with. I'm too tired to think of any other numbers. Give us the answer, and I'll check later to see if your guess was right."

"Do you still remember the result you've got?" she asked the postman.

He nodded.

"Am I right to say it was... 9?"

The postman nodded again.

"That was the answer for both of you, by the way," she smiled.

"How would you know if I never told you my number!?" the block president protested.

"The answer is always 9, no matter what number you pick."

6
NONSENSE

"No matter what number I pick? What nonsense is that!? Anyway... rest assured I shall check later. Now my head is too cabbaged." The block president gave a weary sigh. "Was there anything else?"

"Well, yes," the girl nodded. "As I told you before, I came to talk about the announcement."

"Right, the announcement..." The block president raised an important head, then quickly shook it instead: "If it's about the lilac tree, the matter is out of my hands. The tree is not lucrative enough, it only blooms for a few weeks in the spring, and the committee members have unanimously decided it has to come down."

"That's a shame, really, but the reason why I'm here is actually what was stated below that. The footnote."

"Ah... the cabbage issue. I see. Well, since you are new in the building and don't know how we do things here on Lavender Street, this time you'll get off with just a warning."

"A warning!" The exclamation slipped from her lips before she could do anything to prevent it. "I only picked a few cabbages from the block's allotment. Isn't that what a collective garden is there for?"

"Did you use your cabbage ration card?"

"No, I wasn't even aware there was such a thing," she shrugged.

"Well, miss, there is."

"In that case, could you please tell me where I can get one?"

"The duty of handing out the cabbage cards falls upon the block president" the host recited proudly.

"Then why didn't you give me a ration card?" she said in a bewilderedly amused tone of voice.

"Because you never asked for one. Anyway, here you are." He produced a blank slip of paper from his pocket and handed it to her. "From now on I hope you shall obey the rules, young lady, and stop helping yourself to the block cabbages willy-nilly," he cautioned, flashing a good-humoured fatherly smile.

"I didn't steal anything," the girl heard herself say, wondering if perhaps this was all just a silly, poorly-written and slightly comical fantasy.

"How many cabbages did you pick?"

"I don't know exactly. A rowful. But I replaced them with flowers and seeds."

"Flowers don't fill one's belly, miss. Can you cook?"

"Not really," she laughed. "But I'm good at heating up ready meals."

It was the easy answer. In truth, she could once cook – she knew it in her heart – but her cooking had involved something or someone she could no longer remember.

"Well, miss," the block president countered, "let me tell you that one cabbage is enough for a talented and conscientious housewife to feed her family for a week. Did you eat all the cabbages you picked?"

"No, sir, I didn't," she answered, sounding to her own ears like a respectful cadet. "I sold them at the market instead."

"There you go. That's illicit commerce added to theft. Consider yourself lucky to get off with a simple warning." The block president exhaled a contented sigh. "There, I'm glad we settled the matter. In fact, let's drink to that!" He raised his mug and added cheerfully: "Here's to cordial relations between neighbours!"

A few minutes later, seeing his guests to the door, the block president asked the girl to remind him the steps of that maths trick of hers.

"It's not my trick, I just read it in a book. Anyway... Pick any one or two-digit number, multiply it by 2, add 18, divide the sum by 2 and then subtract the number you thought of initially. Shouldn't you maybe write this down?"

"No need," the perfect host replied. "I've got it all memorized."

7
BEFORE WE WERE INTERRUPTED

"Before we were interrupted," the girl turned towards the postman as they were coming down the stairs together, "when you were telling me about the town's history, you seemed to presume I wasn't aware of it."

"And was I right?"

"Somewhat, yes. I don't know… Something happened and I forgot a lot of things."

He smiled at her. "I'm only trying to help you remember."

8
NOT EVEN CLOSE

All energy of his official capacity vanished, the block president threw his uniform jacket on the back of a chair and crumpled down onto the sofa. Pick a number... Let's see... 18. Divide it by 2. Nine. Subtract 18. Minus 9. Multiply by 2. Minus eighteen. And now add the initial number. Zero. What did she say the answer was? 9? Not even close!

The girl returned to her flat on the second floor and spent the rest of the day feeling rotten. That's what seemed to happen every time she stepped out of her world and ventured into the real one. Somehow she'd always end up doing or saying the wrong thing and then she'd feel guilty about it. And that's exactly how she felt right now. Even if her brain told her it was an absurd accusation, maybe the block president was right after all. Maybe she was, indeed, a thief.

That night she dreamt of a big fish tank set in the middle of a tiny room, almost filling it entirely. The two upper layers of water were like a gladiators' arena. To defend themselves against the predatory species, some of the smaller fish puffed up to ten times their size, others fought with their sharp spines, some hid in crevices, trying to make themselves invisible and, at the opposite pole, others paraded in bright colours, advertising their deadly poison. On the bottom, in the deep murky waters few dared explore, a blind fish swam peacefully, smoking a cigar.

The following morning, as usual, the girl put on a nice dress, and went to water the flowers and seeds in the cabbage garden. This time she did it almost resentfully though. She shouldn't have planted them in the first place. But she had, and now she was responsible for them.

Duty fulfilled, the girl put down her watering can and headed for the supermarket around the corner to get some cocoa. She needed a warm comforting drink.

9
GOOD ADVICE, IN ALL

Next thing she knew, she was sitting at the pub with a ruddy-faced old man, drinking beer. They sat for the longest time in silence, people watching. And then she poured her heart out to him.

"So you're a cabbage thief. Big deal." The playful sparkle in the old chap's eyes, which might've been simply induced by alcohol, gave away the mischievous little boy hiding in that wrinkled body of his. "If anything, that makes you even more likeable."

"But technically speaking, I didn't *steal* those cabbages," she objected. "You see, there are 1248 rows of cabbages in the garden and only 15 flats."

The ruddy-faced old fellow eyed her merrily. "How much is that in all, love – cabbage-wise?"

"I don't really know," the girl confessed, feeling even guiltier that she'd never actually counted the total number of cabbages in the garden. But in her defence, that would've taken forever. Probably. More or less. "All I know is that there are one thousand two hundred and forty-eight rows, which doesn't even make sense …"

"That's not what I meant, petal." The old man took a satisfied sip from his pint and chuckled. "Anyway, who cares how many flats, and how many cats, and how many rows, and how many cauliflowers in each row?"

"Cabbages," she conscientiously amended.

"What's that?" he said absent-mindedly.

"For some strange reason, they happened to be cabbages, not cauliflowers," the girl explained, meaning to tell him about the mystery of the incongruously named street she inhabited, in the hope that given his age, the old man might perhaps be able to shed some light on the matter.

But he patted her on the head instead, like a good-humoured granddad, and simply said:

"So you nicked a few cabbages. It's not much of a theft, pet, all things considered."

"But I planted something else instead," she felt the urge to remind him, yet again.

"There you go. You took a row and made it your own. Good girl!" The old man scribbled something on a napkin, then handed it to her and stood up, slightly unsteady on his feet. "Here's something to help you along on your quest. And, for pity's sake, petal, loosen up. Stop taking yourself so seriously!"

Those very words must have been the help he meant. Whatever the wise and mischievous old boy had written on the napkin was gibberish. Nevertheless, the girl stuck the napkin in her pocket and then, remembering what she'd set off for in the first place, continued on to find a grocery.

10
MODERATION AND CREATIVITY

The Moderation & Creativity grocery store was a huge place packed with shelves which seemed to be bulging with merchandise. In fact, on closer inspection, one could tell all that abundance consisted of only three types of products, displayed in vast quantities, with an almost military precision, again and again, on every available surface. This week it was crackers, tins of beans and tomato juice. A cheerful and explosive combination.

The concept had been introduced years before by a former mayor in an attempt to simplify the life of his fellow citizens by sparing them the stress and confusion of having too many choices and not knowing what to choose. Some considered it a pure stroke of genius. Moderation brought order and peace of mind. It made people more serene and creative. And then they must have run out of creativity, because one day they lost their temper and shot the mayor.

The girl could only vaguely remember the story. In its reinvented present form, the grocery store was now open to the modern public for therapeutic and philosophical purposes. Minimalism made people feel more grounded, more in touch with their inner selves, more free to focus on what really mattered.

Of course, they didn't have any cocoa. It wasn't cocoa week. There was a supermarket close by, a regular one where several different brands of cocoa were probably available at all times, but the girl went straight back to her flat. She had to get back to work.

That evening, the postman brought her a larger than life box of cocoa. It was so big they struggled to get it through the door.

"Who sent it?" the girl asked, laughing confusedly.

"No idea," he laughed along.

They drank hot cocoa in silence, and then the postman stood up. "What are you really looking for?"

"I don't know exactly," she said. "You see, it's all a big blur – some sort of amnesia. I can't remember who I am or what brought me here."

"Maybe it's time you sent someone a postcard."

"I don't have any postcards at hand," she returned, trying to conceal a smile.

"I thought you'd say that. Here you go," the postman smiled back, handing her a picture of the cabbage garden on Lavender Street. "Stop prevaricating. You're looking in all the wrong places. Just listen to your heart. Start with simple, familiar things."

The girl thought for a moment, then wrote a single word on the back of the picture:

HELLO

With a slightly shaking hand, she added in the corner: *To the boy who was selling potted lavender at the market.*

11
MULTIPLE CHOICES

The following morning when she woke up, the postman's words were still ringing in her head. *You're looking in all the wrong places.* But which were the right places? She tried to immerse herself in her work, but she couldn't focus. Maybe that was it. Maybe the key to the puzzle was hidden right there, in her work. There was nothing more real or more familiar in her life. All she had to do was try and put the pieces back together.

Armed with pencil and paper, the girl stacked her books, all the books she'd ever translated, in chronological order. It was a multiple choice exercise with four possible answers:

A) At least one of those books was supposed to point her in the right direction, teach her something important or shed some light on the situation

B) All the books were relevant to her quest

C) None of them was of any consequence to her personal life

D) All of the above

She began with the nonfiction section. *The History of Classical Music*; *Western Painters*; *The Lost Empire*; *Learn to Play Keyboards in Under Three Hours; A Pocket-guide To The North And South; 15 Poets Who Changed the World*; *Fundamental Breathing Techniques*; *45 Fun Maths Tricks*; *Eastern Myths And Mysteries; 90 Chocolate Delights*; *Secrets Of The Deep Sea; Astrology for Beginners*; *The Dog Owner's Bible*; *Love Your Skin*; *The Bible of Beading Techniques*; *Discover Our Planet; Discover Our Galaxy; The Dressmaker's Encyclopaedia; 900 Pies and Tarts.* Her head was already spinning. And then there was all the translated fiction – dozens of novels. Their sheer number was daunting.

Confused and uninspired, the girl wrote down the first thought that came to her mind:

THE TRANSLATOR IS A TIME AND SPACE TRAVELLER.

Thousands and thousands of pages and all the words filling every single page were hers without really belonging to her. How long had it taken to translate all those books and what made her do it in the first place? She wasn't exactly saving lives. Yes, some of those novels had been captivating, well-written and moving – she couldn't and wouldn't deny that. But at the end of the day, none of them were essential to human kind. And if there were any truly crucial books in the world, she knew it would only take as little as a few mistranslated words to fundamentally alter any message, no matter how important.

And yet ...

Whispered chords surged from deep within, washing through her like streams of cool water. For the briefest moment, she could hear the flapping of wings, see a tree standing tall, rooted in the middle of her heart. And then it all disappeared, swept away in the wind.

THE TRANSLATOR IS SELFLESS, she wrote and, blinking at the hazed memory, picked up *The Dressmaker's Encyclopaedia*. That was something she would have loved – to be able to sew her own dresses. But she couldn't even grasp the basics of sewing. That book had been atrocious to translate. As hard as she tried, for the life of her, that was the one time she simply couldn't visualize what she was translating. The translation of each and every technique had felt like a crucifixion. While the words translated easily, their actual meaning escaped her completely. It was like translating from gibberish into gibberish.

The girl picked up a novel, browsed through it and smiled.

FEW UNDERSTAND THE SIGNIFICANCE OF EVERY WORD, NEEDED OR SUPERFLUOUS, EVERY COMMA AND EVERY FULL STOP USED IN A WRITTEN STORY BETTER THAN ITS TRANSLATOR, she wrote, adding underneath: THE TRANSLATOR IS A BOOK'S MOST CONSIDERATE READER.

Focus. Focus, the girl willed herself. Was there anything she had learned from these books? Well, yes. All sorts. How to breathe and smile in her internal organs – that had come in handy at one time of her life, she couldn't exactly remember when, or where, or why; how to make ornamental knots, and that's pretty much where her craftsmanship ended; how history could be changed simply by the way one told it; how to create an astrological chart; the secret powers of crystals; how to housebreak a puppy; how empires would come and go, and so many other useful things that she'd long forgotten.

It was all pointless; this wasn't leading to anything meaningful. The girl sighed and jotted down one more random thought:

A TRANSLATOR IS AN INDIVIDUAL WHO LIVES PARALLEL LIVES.

For some reason that she couldn't quite grasp yet, those books were her second life. That much was clear. While this world of words still held its secrets, the true mystery was her first, real life. Who was she and what was she doing here?

Tired to try and make sense of it all, the girl erased everything she'd written before and replaced it with the one true certainty she had:

I AM A TRANSLATOR.

Then she went out to get the newspaper.

12
VANDALISM

The headlines announced in bold print: ***Great Grey Wall Vandalized Overnight***. 'Last night', read the article, 'at the cover of darkness, taking advantage of the locals' absence during holiday week, vandals covered a portion of the town wall in graffiti. Judging by the naïve style of their painting, the offenders are presumed to be of a fairly young age.' When the girl looked at the picture taken at the crime scene, the air rushed from her lungs.

In the middle of the Great Grey Wall, someone had painted, with childish playfulness, a field. An immense, breathtakingly beautiful lavender field.

Speechless, the girl stared at the picture and then something completely unexpected happened. For the first time since she was lost, the tears came. Great heavy tears silently rolling down her cheeks.

When the girl returned to her flat, she found a letter in the post box. A white sheet of paper containing three simple words:

I AM HERE.

That weekend, returning home from the mountains and the sea coast, the Chesternutters were appalled to find their Great Grey Wall partly coloured up. In truth, more than anything, they were disappointed. There was a wall drawing competition coming up soon and whoever the vandals were had partly spoilt the sportive competitors' fun. Not dejected however, a handful of hands-on citizens brought a big tub of grey paint, armed themselves with paintbrushes, and by the following Monday the wall was as good as new. A perfect grey, empty canvas.

13
THAT TAKES THE BISCUIT

The girl kept tending to her row of flowers and seeds. Every day she would spend a little more time in the garden, watering, weeding and simply enjoying being around them. Every day she'd feel a little bit more confident, a little bit less out of place. So much so that now she dared occasionally raise her eyes and look at the active fashionista's flat on the first floor, the only flat in the building that had see-through glass walls, inviting everybody to sneak a peek and see whatever the occupant was doing. Most of the times, the fashionista would just sit on the sofa, looking bored, which was in fact of great help. This way the girl could focus on her gardening without getting distracted. The four varieties of lettuce she'd started from seed were already beginning to sprout.

Wherever she went, the girl from the second floor carried, stashed in her pocket, two sheets of paper – the one reminding her she was not alone, and another to help her remember who she was. On the latter she would write down things she was randomly discovering along the way. It was Thursday when she wrote: WORDS HAVE MAGICAL POWERS. THEY SHOULD BE HANDLED WITH CAUTION. Something told her it was true, but the girl didn't have a clue what it really meant. All she knew was that she liked words. She liked how they looked and she liked how they'd sound. Especially those little quirky, mischievous ones that sometimes played hide and seek with her for hours or even days on end, hiding behind curtains, under the bed, in the cupboard, among dresses that hung on coat hangers for too long, unworn. Eventually she'd give up searching and just leave a blank space on the page, when suddenly they'd pop up, laughing and shaking their head.

Yes, she liked words. The girl smiled, and that's when a neighbour joined in and quietly helped her with the weeding. It was the rich man who lived on the ground floor. Rumours had it he'd won the lottery years before. For some strange reason though, the lottery winner kept working as an accountant and living in his humble flat on Lavender Street. On holiday, he'd go exploring the four corners of the earth, every year joining ever more complex and gruelling expeditions. The rich explorer from Lavender Street had even been on the telly a few times, talking about his travels around the world, but he'd never actually said what he was really looking for, and the telly watchers didn't have a clue, and most of them couldn't care less, whether he'd found it or not.

The girl from the second floor didn't know all these things. She was just grateful for the man's quiet help and company. If anything, that's what her solitary row of flowers had achieved: it made her come out of her shell and interact with people.

On her way up to her flat, she met the block president, who was hurriedly coming down the steps, taking two at a time. In front of her, he stopped short and declared sternly:

"That trick of yours doesn't work. It's utter rubbish."

It took the girl a moment to realise what he was talking about. "Did you follow the exact instructions I gave you?" finally came the words she said out loud.

"I did indeed. And the answer is not nine, as you said. It's zero. Zero, zilch, zip, nada, nothing." The block president took a deep flustered breath, and then flashed a benevolent smile. "From now on I'd suggest we all stick to what we know, young lady. To evident, well-established, logical truths, like 1+1=2. One biscuit plus another biscuit always equals two biscuits." With that, he patted her on the shoulder and left, smiling broadly.

The girl returned to her flat, craving biscuits. Strangely, this time she didn't feel either guilty or mortified. The block president had just called her a liar and she wasn't at all bothered. Instead, she took a dictionary, looked up the word *axiom*, and then wrote down:

In ancient philosophy, a statement so evident it was accepted as true without controversy or question. In modern logic, simply a premise or starting point for reasoning. The word comes from the Greek *axiōma* and initially its meaning was slightly different from that of the word *postulate*. Eventually the difference was lost in translation and the two terms became synonymous.

She erased the last two sentences and, leaving an empty space, added underneath:

In this context zero is agreed to be the first one. 1 plus 1 equals 2 because it has to. It's a necessary rule in this game of created numbers so that new numbers can be created.

No sooner had the girl written the words down than the postman arrived. He was curious to know how many languages she spoke.

"Six," she replied. "One I was born with, one I inherited, one is the way I feel and think, and the others were gifts I hid in a safe place and no longer remember where."

14
THE SCRIBE'S DAUGHTER

In a great city there once lived an old scribe whose family came from a distant land.

He ran his business in the central square, recording receipts and inventories, assisting various commercial transactions, settling disputes, and writing the occasional letter for the illiterate customer. Every now and again some high official would come for him, and the old scribe would disappear for weeks on end. That's when he was copying secret manuscripts, and he had to say out loud each word he was writing down, and there were sacred words he would have to cleanse his entire body before transcribing. After the resulting scrolls were proofread and accepted, they would to be buried or hidden away in remote caves.

In a land where few could read or write, scribal services were in great demand. Work was always abundant, and with work came money and status. Nonetheless, the scribe lived a simple and private life, devoting every spare moment to the one person he held most dear in the whole world, the only family he had left – his young daughter.

When she was ready, he taught her all he knew. They came from a long line of master scribes and that's how they passed on the secrets of their art from one generation to the next, over the millennia.

At first, the man tested his daughter's natural skills. Before she could talk, he gathered a few things and playfully placed them all in front of her – an array of mysterious toys to choose from. Among them, there was a clay tablet, a bowl of mouth-watering fruits, an eye-catching necklace, a small, artfully carved horse, a pile of sparkling silver, and a plain reed stylus. Without hesitation, his daughter picked up the stylus and, pressing it onto the clay tablet, started humming a song. Her choice would've been enough to prove she had the calling. It was the tune that intrigued her father. Out of curiosity, the man looked at the clay tablet, expecting to see just some childish doodling. When he saw the clearly drawn symbol, the air rushed from his lungs. Then he breathed in and smiled.

Her vocation once confirmed, the old scribe waited patiently, letting his daughter laugh, run and play, happy and carefree. He didn't have to rush. He knew life's deepest mysteries only reveal themselves through the joy and innocent eyes of a child. This joy was a precious gift, a secret gateway that his daughter needed to experience first-hand so she could find and recognise it later on.

The years passed and when the time came, her father began her training with the simplest of truths.

"Knowledge is power, my child, but knowledge without wisdom is joyless nothingness." The scribe paused for a moment and looked into his daughter's big brown eyes. "Wisdom is only achieved when your heart meets the heart of things. And when all wisdom is gone..." He took a wooden stick and wrote something in the dirt. "Remember this?"

The girl nodded with a smile. She didn't remember the day, but she knew it was the first symbol she ever drew.

"When all wisdom is gone," her father repeated, "all we have left to fight off the darkness is what this sign stands for."

Under his guidance, the girl learned to prepare the two colours their forerunners used on clay tablets, papyrus and wood. She learned a secret recipe for a special black ink, and how to use clean animal skin to write on and bind manuscripts with.

One day, her father told her how long ago, scribes worked with painters and artisans to decorate buildings and monuments with artwork and hieroglyphic text. "Our ancestor, Ninsar, the royal scribe's daughter, fell in love with one of the painters," he said, and showed her the love poems Ninsar had carved into wood hundreds of years before their time, signing the ones her lover never got to see as Bendis, the name of her sorrow. He knew his daughter would have liked to find out how and why that had come to be, but she was still too young to hear the full details of their ancestor's heartbreaking story. "The king – the one Ninsar's father worked for – died in a battle," he therefore changed the perspective, "and the man who killed him became the new ruler of the land. They called him The Great Boasting Bull, because he had all the inscriptions about his defeated opponent removed, and replaced with ones praising his own glory. Sometimes, history is just a point of view."

15
THE STRAWBERRY PICKER

The block of flats on Lavender Street was a five story high building, including the ground floor, with three humble abodes on each landing. In one of the flats from the top floor lived a woman whom everybody called *the strawberry picker*. Her story was as mysterious as it was simple. She used to teach Geography and Moonscience at the local elementary school, and then one day, out of the blue, the teacher quit her job and off she flew, to pick strawberries in a sunny faraway land. Nobody knew why, and she never talked about it.

She must have had some sort of epiphany, the mystical ones suggested, optimistically. Or maybe it was, in fact, an act of rebellion, snapped back, crushing their argument flat, a fistful of rebels without a cause, getting a round of applause. Perhaps she was running away from something, joined in a group of joggers, looking over their shoulders. Eventually, an environmentalist held up a hand and offered with flair, ready to make a stand: What if she simply wanted a change of scenery? A breath of fresh air?

Be that as it may, after ten years of picking strawberries in a faraway land, the woman returned to her hometown, moved back into her old flat on Lavender Street and became a consultant. What kind of advice she provided, in what field or to whom, was something she didn't care to share with anybody in the building. The first neighbour who discovered her secret happened to be the girl living on the second floor.

They met for the first time on Friday morning. As usual, the girl was out in the garden, watering her row of flowers and seeds that the strawberry picker had never noticed before. The windows of the latter's flat on the fourth floor gave onto the other side of the building and, not caring much for the cabbage garden, the woman usually just ignored it. This time however, on passing by, something made her stop and turn her eyes.

That's how she spotted that solitary row of flowers. It looked so raw, so clumsy and endearingly out of place, plonked as it was right there in the middle of the block's garden for everybody to see, the strawberry picker couldn't help but smile. She would've probably done something outrageous like that when she was younger. Or perhaps she might when she'd be older. Either way, she understood.

Half an hour later, the two of them were sat at the kitchen table in the strawberry picker's flat on the top floor, drinking pear and caramel tea.

Silently, the hostess searched her guest's face and smiled a warm, knowing smile. "Have you been through my_?" She paused for a moment and decided it wasn't time yet. "Have you been through the woods?"

"No, I haven't," the girl said somewhat puzzled, involuntarily straightening her hair. "As a matter of fact, today I only went downstairs to water the flowers. It's on my to-do list, though. I hear there are some really nice woods around here. Why do you ask?"

"It's just that you are a bit older than I thought." The strawberry picker laughed. "I'm tired and blabbering. Pay no mind to me, honey – you look lovely. Young and lovely."

The girl didn't know what to say. The mixed feedback she'd been receiving on the matter in the last couple of weeks, or days, was a bit confusing.

They went on talking about all sorts: roses, breathing techniques, music, arts, past wars, winter sports. The girl had a vast knowledge of miscellaneous things, accumulated from all the books she'd translated, and all the specialty books she'd studied as research for her translations, on subjects that more often than not wouldn't have interested her otherwise, and all the books she'd read about things she was genuinely interested in, and others she read just because she liked reading, and all the books that came beforehand, teaching her how to read, comprehend and decipher all books. She could talk about virtually anything but herself. If her brain worked as a huge data library, she figured that at the last required cleanup, in order to avoid information overload, it must've randomly cleared all personal data and memories, leaving her with a jumble of dispersed, gratuitous information, all useless and irrelevant to her personal history.

"Pity we don't have any biscuits to dunk in our tea," the strawberry picker sighed eventually, and then her eyes lit up. "Let's pay a visit to the ballerina who lives on the third floor! She makes the best pies in town." Smiling, the woman stood up and took the girl's arm. "And who knows? If we ask nicely, she might give us a coffee reading too."

16
FALSE FRIENDS

The ballerina lived in the flat opposite the block president's and, perhaps by way of proximity, her living room was very reminiscent of his. Except for the absence of the embroidered wall carpet, there was the same multitude of lace doilies, similar looking bookshelves and the same display cabinet, filled with porcelain figurines. The drunkards' section was missing, but the ballerinas, dainty ladies and the mixed Zoo were all there.

"I know they are old and tacky, but I guess I'm emotionally attached to them," the lady of the house explained, between fetching plates, cups and teaspoons, and watching that the coffee brewing on the cooker didn't foam up and spill over. "But I'm taking these to the flea market," the hostess added when she returned with pie and knife, pointing to the robust pair of pigeons, tiger on the prowl and glass fish set on a side table. "They are too clunky even for me," she chortled.

When the ballerina had opened the door, the girl from the second floor had expected to set eyes on a tall, slender creature with elegant poise and a nose gracefully stuck in the air. Instead, she found herself staring at a small plump old dear with a broad smile on her face, and a heart full of cheer.

"It's apple and cinnamon cake," the hostess chimed, cutting a few slices and setting them on three delicate desert plates. "Tuck in," she said with a happy chuckle before rushing back to the kitchen to check on the coffee.

The girl felt a shiver down her spine and suddenly a memory emerged from a deep forgotten place. Apple and cinnamon cake. That used to be her favourite. She couldn't remember when or why, but one thing was certain – this cake looked and smelled the same as the apple cake she once loved. She held her breath for a moment, then took a mouthful and chewed slowly, with her eyes closed, willing the memories back. They didn't come. False friends, silently concluded the translator. Words in two languages which, while looking or sounding similar, differed significantly in meaning. The old ballerina's cake was scrumptious. That's probably why the whole town loved the pies and cakes she baked. But even though her apple and cinnamon cake looked and smelled like the one the girl remembered, it didn't taste exactly the same.

The cheerful hostess returned with the coffee pot and filled three small white cups with the steaming brew. "Make a wish," she said, before they all took a first sip from the thick bubbly drink.

The girl could have wished to remember everything she'd forgotten – her past, who she was, what had brought her here and what it was she'd been looking for. But she didn't.

"After we've enjoyed our coffee together, leave the last mouthful in," the lady of the house warmly instructed, "and carefully swirl the grounds around to nicely cover the inside of the cup, then turn the cup over onto the saucer."

And with that, rather unexpectedly, the ballerina jumped up and danced for a minute around the room, finishing off with a few pirouettes. She was surprisingly sprightly for her age, her dedication verging on adorable.

At the end of the dance performance, the two guests applauded and cheered, and the little old woman curtsied gracefully. Watching her, the girl remembered that old local saying – *The sword won't fall upon a bowed head.* Suddenly the angle had changed and the meaning took a new shape. She looked one more time at the small ballerina who was still curtsying; head bowed deeply, kooky, radiant, humble and grateful. In this new context there was no cowardice in the bow, just a heartbreaking innocence, and the only thing out of place was the sword. The sword made no sense; it was just cruel and gratuitous.

"Force of habit," the hostess said apologetically, slightly out of breath but beaming. "Please, feel free to look around!" she exclaimed, tracing her younger guest's gaze. "My house is a museum that loves visitors."

The girl stood up and went to check out her elderly neighbour's book collection. The ones on the top shelves were all cookery books. She had a closer look, hoping to find the two she'd translated. They weren't there. The ballerina's cookbooks were all old, with yellowed, over-turned pages. The girl took one from the shelf and quickly browsed though. The recipes listed the exact amounts of the required ingredients, but the instructions were rather vague, leaving much to the reader's skill, experience and imagination.

"Have more cake," the hostess begged, then promptly apologized: "It's nothing to write home about, I used cinnamon powder from the Moderation & Creativity grocery, and it's not exactly the best in the world. I go there every now and again – for old times' sake more than anything. And to feel rich," she added with a chuckle. "It's the only supermarket in town that sells less than my money can buy." They all laughed and her two guests assured her the cake was delicious. In fact, they each helped themselves to one more slice.

"You could come with me to the flea market this Sunday," the ballerina suggested, smiling hopefully. "One can find all sorts of little treasures there. Look what I found last time!" She pointed merrily at a vintage looking small television set in the corner. "It's black and white – it takes me back to the days of my youth." She checked the coffee cups. "All right, girls, it's time to flip them onto your saucers."

While they waited for the coffee grounds to settle, the lady of the house went on telling them one story after the other, about the days when she was young and things were different and, beyond the black and white, it took some doing to see the future bright. Her two guests were listening intently, both knowing better than to interrupt her with unnecessary questions. This was the lovely old ballerina's time. Her time to shine and share her stories. The two younger women weren't listening just out of politeness. One of them knew the other needed to hear what was being said.

"And that's how the mayor who gambled away the town's money came up with the idea," the ballerina concluded, carefully picking up one of the cups. "I think we can get to the reading now."

The strawberry picker checked her watch and stood up. "I'm sorry, ladies, but I have to go. Business meeting in ten minutes," she explained, heading for the front door.

The translator followed her half-heartedly. It was the polite thing to do; the hostess looked a little tired now, but deep down the girl would have loved to stay, just a bit longer. The ballerina's flat might have looked similar to the block president's, but unlike his, hers didn't feel strange and obsolete. It felt warm, cosy and welcoming.

Seeing them to the door, the old dear whispered in her ear:

"Don't worry, sweetheart. I'll read yours and tell you all about it next time we see each other."

More than anything, it sounded like a silent plea. The girl smiled and nodded.

"See you tomorrow," the strawberry picker called back before disappearing into the lift.

17
PATIENCE

Later that day the girl met the postman and told him all the new things she'd learned about the town's history. "I think I found a new meaning to that old saying," she concluded. "This has obviously never been a war-faring town. They are peaceful, gentle people who just want to mind their own business and get along with everybody."

The postman didn't say anything.

"Have they ever invaded any other town?" the girl asked, determined to make a point.

He shook his head.

"So they've always been the invaded ones," she recapped quietly. "And they learned how to deal with it. Submissive gene, not a trace of rebellious spirit in their DNA."

The postman chuckled. "I wouldn't jump to conclusions, if I were you. Have you remembered anything else since we last met?"

She shook her head. "But as for that local saying, I think I have now figured it out."

"As a translator, when can you honestly say you truly know what a book is about?" the postman countered.

"You know, at times you can actually judge a book by its cover," the girl smirked. "All right, all right, point taken. I'll just have to be patient and take it one step at a time."

They finished their cocoa in silence, and then the postman left.

That night, the girl did what she'd been doing every evening for the past week or so: she wrote to Lavender Boy. She would write to him at night, and the following morning she'd find his answer in the mailbox. Lavender Boy. It didn't sound very manly, but that was all right. They were both young and secretly wild, two childlike souls who spoke the same tongue. Her mother's or one of the others. It didn't matter which one it was. She felt at home and safe in their language.

The boy now lived in a faraway town. He must've moved there after he'd painted that field of lavender on the great wall, most probably due to the inexplicable lack of interest shown by the citizens of Chesternutville in potted herbs. Be that as it may, every day, from afar and yet feeling so near, he sent her humorous little poems which made her laugh, scribbled on the back of quaint little drawings which made her smile. It might not have seemed like much to some, but to the girl who lived on the second floor in that old block of flats from Chesternutville, who'd almost forgotten how to laugh and smile, those silly little poems and childish doodles, gentle and healing as they were, meant the world.

18
CHILD'S PLAY

The lessons continued, and the scribe's daughter learned something new every day. She discovered the secrets of current-day writing, as well as the mysteries of old scripts. As child's play, she quickly learned how to solve hieroglyphic puzzles, which read from top to bottom, which from left to right, and which from right to left. "Learn how to put things in the right order," her father said.

Next he introduced to her the less time consuming sacerdotal writing, chosen by priests of old times, and then the even easier signs of the demotic script, used mainly for commerce and shorthand. It was unlikely she'd ever need the latter to make a living, but her father knew the mundane could sometimes equal, if not surpass the generally accepted higher notions.

Simultaneously, the old scribe was educating his daughter in the arts of music, maths, business, science and literature. "Knowing how to read and write is not enough," he told her. "You need to understand what you read or write about."

Each sound, each symbol, the scribe would demonstrate, had its own melody, its own secret taste, its own beat. "Like the one you hummed when you drew that sign into clay."

He taught her how to discover the right key for interpreting Mesopotamian languages. In the oldest, multilingual script he knew, the number of words and meanings represented by each syllable differed greatly from one language to the next. "Something that might appear nonsensical in one language will make sense in another. Always try to find the right context."

The girl learned how to translate written messages, and then her father showed her how to decipher encrypted ones. She learned how to listen to the silence and see the unwritten, how to search her heart and not misinterpret. She learned to speak the language of the universe.

19
THE WISH

That night, after she wrote to Lavender Boy – telling him about the interesting and knowledgeable woman who lived on the fourth floor, and about the old ballerina who could read in coffee grounds, and how the ballerina had asked them to make a wish before turning their coffee cups upside down – the girl closed her eyes and remembered something. It was a most unexpected and vivid memory, but then she fell asleep and forgot all about it.

The following morning she found the boy's reply in the post box. This time there was no doodling, no funny little poems, just one simple question: WHAT DID YOU WISH FOR?

The girl wrote the answer on the same piece of paper, right beneath his question: I WISHED TO BE HAPPY.

Just as she finished writing, the postman knocked on her door and she handed him the letter. "It's for Lavender Boy."

He nodded. "Have you remembered anything else?"

Why did he keep asking the same question? ... She gave him a puzzled look and shook her head. "Since last night, you mean? ... Nothing, really. This morning I woke up with this strange urge to write something down. The words were still clear in my mind. Something about knowledge and wisdom. But then I went to have a shower and the water was very cold at first, and then very hot and it took me ages to adjust it so that it'd be just right, and somewhere along the way all those words in my head became blurred. I tried to put them back together, but I couldn't. All I can think of right now is: if I know so many things and knowledge is power, how come I feel so powerless?"

The postman replied with yet another question he'd asked her before: "How many languages do you speak?"

"Six," the girl repeated her previous answer with a sigh, then suddenly changed her mind. "Or possibly nine. But I don't know how many belong to others and which is exactly mine."

"You're not powerless," the postman smiled. "All the tools you need are at your disposal."

20

ORANGES, BANANAS AND UNICORNS

After the postman left, the girl took a giant ladle, went to the giant box still standing in the middle of her kitchen, almost filling it entirely, and spooned out enough of the contents to fill two smaller, normal sized boxes, one with orange, and the other with banana flavoured cocoa.

First she went to the fourth floor and knocked on the door, but there was no answer. Since the strawberry picker wasn't at home, the girl gave both boxes of cocoa to the old ballerina, who was more than happy to see her again. She opened the door wearing what looked like a pair of children's sunglasses with lime green lenses.

"Today I fancied watching the telly in a different colour," the old lady chuckled. "Oh, by the way – come and see!" She urged the girl to step inside and led the way to the living room. "Our neighbour is on. It's one of those travel programs."

It was indeed the rich man who lived on the ground floor, talking about the latest expedition he'd been on.

"Do you have any hobbies?" the girl heard the reporter ask.

"I like to play the saxophone," replied the explorer.

A book she'd once translated came to her mind. *Learn How To Play Keyboards In Under Three Hours.* No, she'd never tried. Then the girl remembered another book, the first one she'd ever translated, *The History of Classical Music.* While working on the translation, she had listened to all that music, old and new, and some of it had a healing effect she would've never even dreamed to expect. The music had awakened something in her, the memory of a secret language she'd long forgotten, one that had nothing to do with the words she was translating.

"Do you take it with you on your travels?" the reporter's voice resounded from the telly.

The explorer smiled and shook his head. "It would take up too much room, I'm afraid."

The girl pointed to the two boxes of cocoa the ballerina had set on the coffee table. "One is orange, and the other one is banana flavoured," she explained.

"Oranges and bananas!" exclaimed the hostess. "Oh dear, I remember the days when they were only available once a year, right before Christmas. Luxury goods, they were. At times, the staff from the supermarket didn't even get to unload the cargo. People would queue up on the spot right there, at the back of the orange and banana truck. Once I stood in a queue for as long as a day or two. And I don't even like oranges, mind you. Never have."

"Which are the three things you'd never travel without?" the reporter's voice broke into their conversation.

"A special talisman, a very loud whistle and a song," the explorer said.

"I love bananas though," the old ballerina went on. "They were still green when we bought them and we'd store them on old newspapers, up on the cupboard, waiting until they were ripe." She laughed softly. "Well, that's how we socialized back then, whether we liked it or not. Standing in queues."

"I reached both the North and the South Pole," sounded the explorer's voice, "I crossed the driest deserts, I climbed the highest mountains and I sailed the deepest seas. In forever young and untamed faraway lands, I met the most joyful people in the world – the wisest there could ever be. And through them, I learned the true meaning of being free."

"Bit of pie, dear?" the ballerina asked cheerfully, already cutting a slice. "Which reminds me! Have you heard about the unicorn meat scandal?" The girl shook her head. "It's all over the news," moaned the lady of the house. "We've put our foot in it one more time!"

"What do you mean? How? What happened?"

The ballerina handed her the newspaper and the girl quickly scanned through the article.

Apparently, Chesternutville exported unicorn meat which, in the past couple of months, had been sold all over the continent by several supermarkets and fast food chains, labelled as beef. The world was up in arms and the international finger was pointed accusingly at the main culprit least likely to give it a back-slap – Chesternutville.

The girl was shocked. "You people eat… unicorns!?"

"I personally don't," the ballerina whimpered apologetically, her bottom lip starting to quiver. "Or well, to be honest... I have. Once, after the war and once in the Moderation & Creativity era... Food was scarce and we were hungry." Distraught, the little old woman buried her face into her hands and broke into sobs. "Oh, I'm sorry... I'm so sorry! I'm an awful human being!"

The translator responded the only way she knew how. Discarding all judgments based on her first impressions, she dealt with the context at hand. Crushed under the weight of the world she was carrying on her frail shoulders, the quaint little ballerina who sat crying miserably next to her now looked even smaller. So the girl did the only thing she could under the circumstances: she awkwardly gave that small sobbing frame a hug. She'd worry about the bigger picture later.

21
NINE STONES

"Why don't you send me to scribal school?" the girl asked her father one day.

"They only accept boys", the old scribe replied. "But what I teach you reaches far beyond anything formal education could ever offer or hold. Remember you come from a long line of master scribes."

"Like the scribe you once told me about, the one who worked for a king?"

"Our ancestors were not only royal scribes. More often than not, they were of royal blood themselves. Sons and daughters of rulers and kings."

"Were there any female scribes among them?"

Her father slowly nodded his head. "Princesses, queens, royal slaves and high priestesses, all remarkable women. One of them moved to a faraway land and became a goddess."

"A goddess!" the girl gasped.

Her father smiled. "Yes, the legendary Bendis."

"Bendis, the royal scribe's daughter – the one who fell in love with the painter that worked with her father?"

"Yes. The painter died and Bendis couldn't bear living without him. So she died too and then was reborn in a distant land, as a goddess."

The girl would've liked to find out how the whole thing worked, how women could die and become goddesses, but before she could say anything her father continued. "Whether male or female, all our ancestors had the calling. A special gift." He gathered nine stones, placed them in the shape of a square, and then began writing symbols on each one. "They could read the written and the untold, they wrote and rewrote, found meanings hidden in the dark and shed light on misinterpretation. They were translators and became creators. And that's what I'm teaching you to do."

By this time each of the nine stones set in the square before him contained a different number of signs, ranging from one to nine, each written in a different script.

"These words, combined, hold a secret meaning," the old scribe said, pointing to the square. "Now let's play a game". He scrambled the message and threw the stones in nine different directions. "Find the pieces and reconstruct the square."

22
MURKY WATERS

"Will you still come with me to the flea market tomorrow?" the ballerina asked in a small voice after she calmed down somewhat, holding tight a tiny, old and ragged, grey teddy bear.

The girl nodded and gave her one more reassuring hug. She needed to get back to her translating, but there was something about this place that, just as the first time, made her want to stay just a little bit longer. It might have been the old ballerina's lavender perfume, or the cheap floral clock hanging on the wall, with pink hydrangea blooms and rosemary painted in the middle, or the soft cushions embellished with patchwork terriers and embroidered roses, or that scented cat shaped candle that had obviously never been lit. *It must've been some special present.* Or maybe the old lady was just attached to cat shaped candles. Just like she was to that threadbare little teddy bear that seemed to be such an earnest and dedicated cuddler.

The girl from the second floor couldn't quite put her finger on it, but there was something in that quaint mishmash of knickknacks and family heirlooms, maybe all of it, that made her feel at home.

"Are you seeing the strawberry picker today?" the old woman's voice broke into her reverie.

"I'm sorry... Who?"

"The strawberry picker. Your friend from the fourth floor."

"Ah... I don't know, really." The girl finally willed herself to stand up and started towards the door.

"If you meet her, make sure you say hello for me."

The girl nodded with a smile and went to the garden to water her flowers. When, by force of habit, she raised her eyes to see what was going on in the no-secrets flat from the first floor, she spotted the two huge, tastefully crafted posters hanging in the fashionista's floor-to-ceiling windows. One, delicately decorated with sparkling glitter in several different colours, read 'UNICORN MURDERERS', while the other, adorned with lace and frills, offered a prompt solution: 'SAVE

THE UNICORNS'. In the background, the activist fashionista was rearranging her walk-in wardrobe.

Gardening routine over, it was time for the translator to return to her translation. On her way back to her flat, wondering whether her translating could be, in fact, some kind of therapy, the girl found Lavender Boy's letter in the post box.

Confused, she wanted to check her watch, but she didn't have one. For some reason, Lavender Boy was breaking their mailing pattern and that made her feel somewhat uneasy. Patterns were her security blanket. They brought order into her otherwise random life.

She put the letter aside and tried to focus on the book she was translating. But the letter was already there and, even if that was the rule, she couldn't wait till the following morning to open it. Eventually, unable to ignore it any longer, the girl picked the letter up and slowly unfolded it.

It was the same plain sheet of paper they'd used the last couple of times. She read the first two lines again.

WHAT DID YOU WISH FOR?

I WISHED TO BE HAPPY, she'd answered.

Below, in slightly bigger letters, he'd now added one more question:

ARE YOU HAPPY THERE?

The girl didn't know exactly how to respond to that. She wasn't *un*happy. The answer would've been somewhere in the grey area between yes and no, but those waters were too deep and murky for her to dare dive into yet. So instead, she wrote back telling him about the book she was translating, how its very simplicity was so challenging at times, and how at some point it felt like she'd stopped the translation and was now writing the story herself.

She looked up from the paper and spotted the cat sunbathing lazily on the window sill, and then the old ballerina came to mind, inspiring a new paragraph in her letter. 'I'm getting to know the locals a little better. Every day I'm learning new things about their history. They seem to suffer from some sort of genetically transmitted form of submissiveness. Maybe I'm here to help them become more confident,' she wrote, involuntarily fashioning a partial possible answer to his question, 'which is a bit ironic given my own lack of self-confidence.'

The girl posted the letter and then went to buy strawberries.

23
THE RIGHT ONE

"When combined, these words written in nine different scripts hold a secret meaning," the scribe said, pointing to the square. "Now let's play a game". He scrambled the message and threw the stones in nine different directions. "Find the pieces and reconstruct the square."

The scribe's daughter found eight of the nine stones and though she searched everywhere for the missing piece of the puzzle, she simply couldn't find it.

"Why did you throw the stones away?" she asked her father.

"To make you look for them," he said smiling. "You searched through hundreds of lookalike stones and found the ones you needed. This is how you learn to be thorough and discerning."

"And now what? I'm still missing one."

"It doesn't matter. Start working with what you have."

The girl translated the symbols written on each stone, and then, using a plain pebble to replace the missing piece, she arranged and rearranged the stones several times in the shape of a square, until they formed an intelligible sequence. The one that would've revealed the exact meaning of the message was the plain pebble lying in the middle of the top row. To its right there was a stone with two signs, and to its left, one with four. Each of the other six stones in the two rows below contained a different number of symbols.

The old scribe took three more stones and wrote four symbols on one, seven on the second and nine on the third. Then he handed them to his daughter. "Choose the one that is missing from the square."

The girl translated the signs on all three. Each translation would've fitted in the middle of the top row, and each assigned a different meaning to the overall message. She was stuck.

"When your mind can't find the answer, look for it in your heart," the old scribe said.

His daughter closed her eyes and listened to the silence. Then she looked at the square of stones set in front of her and she started humming the melody of each set of symbols, gradually merging them together. At first the complete middle and bottom rows, to which she then added the top one, changing melodies for each of the three possible answers. And then she picked one of the three stones and placed it in the centre of the top row.

Her father smiled and nodded. "Yes. That's the right one."

24
A MYSTERIOUS LITTLE SHEEP

Waiting for the traffic lights to turn green, the girl from Lavender Street took a pencil and a crumpled napkin out of her pocket, the one the ruddy-faced old man gave her at the pub, and drew a square:

4		2
3	5	7
8	1	6

She stood staring at the numbers, wondering why the urge to jot them down and why in this particular form, when suddenly a little sheep appeared out of the blue and set to cross the road, causing the stream of traffic to come to a sudden halt in a cacophony of screeching tires and beeping horns. Though confused and frightened by the commotion, the small animal kept going, seemingly determined to reach its destination.

Intrigued, the girl put the napkin back in her pocket and followed the brave little creature to the mall.

The mall parking lot had been cleared of cars and was now filled with a flock of sheep. The girl looked around. No shepherds in sight. In the middle of the parking area she saw a horse and cart and a team of oxen hitched to a massive wagon. Nearby, two men dressed as peasants were posing by an ornamental haystack for the few tourists who had gathered around and were taking pictures. The foldable sign set at the entrance read, simply, ROOTS.

It must be a farmer's market, the girl guessed, approaching the few stalls spread around the place. They were selling honey, homemade jams, syrups, preserves, and cheese wrapped in pine bark. The only non-food stand displayed an array of delicate brooches, each tied to a bow made of a red and white string, with tassels hanging at the two loose ends.

"What are these?" the girl asked the seller, attracted by the daintiness of the small artisanal things.

"Little Marches," the woman said and then, probably taking her for a tourist, went on to explain. "They are lucky charms we offer one another at the beginning of March. To celebrate spring and keep healthy and strong in the coming year. An ancient tradition of ours."

It was long past March. Even so, the girl thought a lucky charm wouldn't do any harm, at any given time. And she could, in fact, do with a bit of good luck right now. In her present circumstances, it seemed she had basically nothing else to rely on. "How much is a Little March?"

"For you, sweetheart, it's free," the vendor replied good-naturedly, handing her a Little March shaped like a four-leaf clover. "A special gift from me."

Speechless and strangely tearful, the girl thanked her with a shaky smile full of surprise and gratitude, and carefully slipped the unexpected tiny present in her pocket, together with her other precious treasures.

Then she glanced around, looking for the little sheep that had brought her there. But it seemed to have disappeared into thin air. The other sheep filling the parking lot were all much bigger and looked much more real. On her way out, the girl had a closer look at the flock. All the sheep were made of cardboard.

25
THE ANSWER IS ALWAYS NINE

It was not long past 1 p.m. The ones who had nine to five jobs were on their lunch break. In the meantime, the conscientious citizens of Chesternutville were protesting in front of the town hall, shouting out slogans such as: *Unicorn murderers! Blood on your hands! You give the Chesternutters a bad name!*

The girl from Lavender Street was just passing by when the mayor stepped outside and addressed the protesters. "Dear fellow citizens," he began, "let it be known that the allegations made against us in the unicorn matter are entirely unfounded. We've never exported unicorn meat labelled as beef."

A sigh of relief passed through the crowd and the mayor continued. "What we did was export unicorn labelled as unicorn, based on contracts which are perfectly legal and can be checked by anyone who wishes to do so. As you all know, here in Chesternutville we have specialized farms where unicorns are raised for slaughter. Our unicorn meat is world renowned. We are all proud of it. But we never, and I repeat, *never*, sold unicorn as beef."

With that, the mayor disappeared back inside, and the protesters, their concerns now alleviated, cheerfully dispersed toward the nearby pubs for a celebratory drink.

The girl took the napkin out of her pocket and stared at the mysterious square of numbers she'd drawn before. Remembering a poem she'd translated, one about multiplying a unicorn by a pear, she then began absent-mindedly adding the three numbers on the right. Fifteen. Then the three on the left. Fifteen. A few more sums and it all became clear. Even the number that was missing from her drawing. She thought of the maths trick she'd tried out in the block president's living room, and smiled. *The answer is always nine.*

And then the girl from Lavender Street suddenly remembered she'd forgotten to buy the strawberries.

26
I DON'T LIKE STRAWBERRIES

Strawberry tray in hand, the girl walked beaming as she revisited the unicorn times a pear poetic equation, and then another poem, written by the same author, gently drifted into her mind. It was a poem she cherished. Someday, the girl decided, she would translate and send it to Lavender Boy. Because it was the way she felt right now. The way you feel when, being lost, you find someone who understands the language of your heart.

She started humming the words like a song:

It's so good that you are, so wondrous that I am!
Two different songs, colliding, intertwining,
Two colours that never met before,
One from down below, turned toward the ground,
The other from high above, almost torn
In this unseen before fiery storm
Of the wonder that you are, and the fortuity that I am.

As she turned into Lavender Street, the strawberry picker caught up with her from behind. "It's a lovely song you're humming," the woman said.

The girl smiled a radiant greeting and held out the tray of strawberries to her. "Here. I got a little prezzie for you. Hope you don't mind."

As the woman walking by her side took the tray, the sky above them suddenly darkened, and what had been a perfectly nice day seemed to drown into nothingness and gloom. But only for an instant or two.

And then the strawberry picker did the most unexpected thing. She threw the tray of strawberries in the nearest bin.

The girl blinked a confused apology. "I'm sorry… I thought you …"

The woman patted her on the shoulder. "It's all right. I know they call me the strawberry picker. But I don't like that name, and I don't like strawberries, as a matter of fact. My name is Bendis."

They walked for a moment in silence, then Bendis spoke again. "When I was a child, I used to love picking strawberries. You see, I grew up surrounded by rules, and being in a strawberry field would feel so liberating. It brought me such joy – to be away from the crowd, away from unsolicited voices that kept telling me how to behave, what to think, how to feel, why and how to be proud." As they rounded the corner, Bendis looked up at the see-through flat on the first floor.

The floor-to-ceiling glass windows still boasted the glittery posters about saving unicorns. The fashionista obviously hadn't heard yet that the matter had been clarified and put to bed, and behind the tastefully decorated protest sheets she was now making pouty faces, taking one selfie after the other.

"I know everybody loves strawberries," Bendis continued her train of thought. "But I don't." Smiling, she took the girl's arm. "Come on. I've got some nice pears for us instead."

27

EVERYTHING MAKES SENSE

Pear in one hand, the girl looked at Bendis apologetically. "Before, when you told me your name, I didn't tell you mine. It's simply because ... I can't remember what it is. You see, something happened and I've forgotten many things. I can no longer remember who I am."

"It's all right. I know."

The statement should have surprised her, but it didn't. For a long moment, the girl looked deeply into Bendis' eyes, as if to somehow find her lost self in them.

"It's not all right," she eventually sighed. "It's all so nonsensical."

Bendis shook her head and began to slice another pear. "Because you're trying too hard to make sense of everything." She smiled wistfully. "In truth, every thing makes sense."

Then why are you so sad, arose the question in the girl's mind. And Bendis answered it, or at least so it seemed. "Because I've lost my ..." She hesitated for a moment. "I've lost my pet."

Suddenly, the doorbell rang and Bendis stood up. "I have a business meeting," she explained, gesturing for the girl to remain seated. "But I want you to stay."

28
THE FLOWER CALENDAR

The young editor wanted to make a good impression. The flower calendar was his first major project, and he knew how much the head of the publishing house valued this woman's opinion. Everything, his entire career, depended on this meeting.

However, he would've expected such a fine and trusted expert to live in a nice house, with a lovely lush garden, not in a place like ... this. By the time he reached the top floor and rang the doorbell, he was out of breath.

Someone came to answer and silently beckoned him in. He couldn't see the person's face, the small hallway was too dark.

Stepping into the kitchen, the young editor found two women sat at the table, eating pears. They somehow resembled each other, as if related. Same dark hair, same dark brown eyes. Though the one wearing a dress looked much younger. Or maybe it was just that look in her eyes, the look of a lost child hiding in a grown-up body. The way he too felt at times. The way he felt right now. Then again, both women had an ageless appearance about them. They could both be either much younger or much older than he imagined. Since he never met the consultant before, the young editor had no idea which of the two she might be. And now, to make matters worse, he'd even forgotten her name.

"Please call me Bendis," magically came to his rescue the older looking woman – the slightly older looking one. No, she was definitely older. Or might it be that…

"Did you bring the pictures?" she asked, as if trying to conceal a smile. Or was it only his imagination? …

What did she just say? Something about cool waters. Why on earth couldn't he focus!?

"The pictures," the woman repeated in an amused tone of voice.

"Ah yes! Yes. The pictures." With fumbling hands, he opened the folder and, staring at her, let the photographs spill out across the table top.

The two women took their time studying each and every picture. Finally they both smiled, and Bendis reached for one of the photos. White peonies against a walnut brown background. "I love the simplicity of this one. It's pure and comforting. What month is it for?"

"March."

"Make it January. That's when the quiet beauty of something soothing is needed. After all the commotion, and heartbreak, and glee, one must step gently into January. What did you have planned initially?"

Why was she talking in rhymes, almost quoting old poems, using words from ancient times? ... Still wondering if this was happening for real, the young editor pointed to the picture of a vibrant bunch of roses set on a sunny terrace, with a lush green garden as a backdrop.

"This would be too taunting, too strident for January," the expert commented. "It's painful to be reminded of the sun's warmth in the grey cold of winter. What do you have for September?"

He lifted his favourite picture. A raw, green field of golden daffodils.

Bendis narrowed her eyes and in that moment a bolt of lightning crossed the cloudless sky. The young editor tried to swallow the lump in his throat, but he couldn't.

"I want you to remember one thing." Though she spoke quietly, he felt a shiver going down his spine. "For as long as you shall live, don't you ever ... Dare. Take. Daffodils. Out. Of. Spring." Her voice was soft, almost whispered, and yet it felt like a deafening scream.

He gave a frantic nod, and Bendis' frown melted into a benevolent smile. "Good job. They are all beautiful pictures. Just make sure everything goes where it belongs. Where it is needed."

29
THEN THAT'S WHAT I SHALL CALL YOU

After the young and now utterly bewildered editor left, both women burst into laughter.

"Wisdom can only be achieved when your heart meets the heart of things," Bendis offered eventually, a voluntary explanation.

It felt good, the girl thought. It felt like having a sister. This world was beginning to feel less and less lonely, less and less foreign. And the daffodils. She could remember seeing the host of golden daffodils in the spring. And now her heart was dancing with them again. Her heart was awakening.

"A long time ago I knew this feeling," Bendis said. "We were too, like in that poem of yours, 'two different songs, colliding, intertwining'."

"It's not my poem. I'm only trying to translate it."

"The music has found you again, that's good. Come on, let me show you something."

Without waiting for an answer, Bendis led the way into the front room and up a narrow staircase. A few seconds later, they were standing on the rooftop.

"This is my secret garden. My heaven on earth."

Looking around, at the trees, the shrubs, the roses, the hydrangeas and the myriad of colourful perennials fluttering in the breeze, the girl gave a gasp of amazement. The enchanted garden appeared to be about ten times the length and width of the actual building, and for some reason, it seemed to float in the air. "I had no idea_"

"Nobody has," retorted Bendis.

"What happened? To the boy you loved."

"The world broke us apart."

A couple of hours later, while feeding the cat that sometimes slept in her hat, the girl remembered something she'd forgotten. So she went back upstairs and knocked on Bendis' door.

"Who is it?" came the woman's voice.

The girl hesitated for a moment. Then she gave the only answer she could. "It's me."

"Then that's what I shall call you."

30

FORTY-FIVE

"You'll call me ... Me?"

"It's a name that suits you."

Taken aback, the girl uttered the first words that came to her mind. "Does your pet happen to be a ... cat?"

"No," Bendis replied. "I don't have a cat."

That night the girl had a strange dream. She was a boy who turned into a man that looked exactly like her. He was the great-grandson of a scribe's daughter, now himself a translator and interpreter. His great-grandmother had taught him all she knew. How to look written words in the eye, listen to their sound, hear the secret beat of what was said and what was left untold, how to breathe in the fragrance of each word, taste its truth in his mouth, then breathe out. She taught him how to shed light in the dark by unravelling translations badly woven and putting the words back together in the right order, according to their rhyme and reason, and then how to unlock any remaining ciphers simply by running it all through his heart.

The young man learned to speak the language of the universe and became an alchemist of sorts: he could take rusty old words and turn them back into gold. When the king gathered the forty-five most illustrious scholars in the land, the young alchemist was one of them. The king placed them in forty-five underground chambers, and asked them all to translate the same collection of writings, without consulting or having any interaction with one another. Each interpreted and translated the manuscript their own way. Some literally, some by paraphrasing, some by rewriting it. No two translations were the same.

The deadline was getting close, and everybody was rushing. Only the young man who looked like her took his time, searching for the unseen, listening to the mysterious chords of the words, breathing them in and feeling their taste on his tongue, then breathing out, until the silent music resounding in his heart spilled over, filling his chamber and the entire underground.

And then the elders of the group got impatient. Breaking the rule set by the king, they secretly gathered together, compared notes and agreed to take action. She ... No, the young alchemist didn't attend the meeting.

With each written sound, the underground was growing darker, and cold, and confusingly loud. His eyes were beginning to hurt. He no longer saw any gold in the words he translated, the writing on the scroll was now covered in mould, the youthful sweetness of early songs turned into the bitter ranting of a disgruntled, exiled old soul. All music was gone, and so was joy. Through the single small window that gave onto the outside, the young alchemist saw a beckoning light. And he followed that sunbeam, leaving it all behind.

Forty-two translators stayed in their cells after he left – she didn't know what had happened to the other two – and by the end, each one translated the writing identically as all the others did.

31
IT'S NOT MY CAT

In the morning, as she was watering her row of flowers and salad greens in the garden, the girl couldn't help but wonder how come she seemed to be a quitter, even in her dreams.

In the meantime, the fashionista was taking yesterday's glittery posters off and replacing them with countless copies of the same book. The unicorn matter was old news. Today's must-have was *The Dressmaker's Encyclopaedia*, the essential read now championed by the mayor's wife.

Oblivious of the fashionista's redecorating activities, the girl raised her eyes, trying to have a glance at the enchanted rooftop garden, but it wasn't there anymore. All she could see were concrete walls, tall and grey.

Suddenly, she remembered. Yesterday, while standing with Bendis on top of the building, in the distance she saw ... the wood. The dark wood that had engulfed her. Where her fragile shell had been shattered into a million pieces, and she lost herself and all her words. And she had to learn them all over again, feeling the weight of each and every one more keenly than ever before. A tear trickled down her cheek. But where was this damned wood? She'd wandered all around town without spotting it once.

"Ahem, miss_," the block president's voice broke into her sorrow.

Quickly wiping her eyes, the girl turned around only to find the tenants' committee gathered before her. Everybody was there, except for the explorer and Bendis. Head bowed, the old ballerina stood on the side, nervously clutching the old threadbare teddy bear in her hands. The silent fashionista was wearing a dress that screamed in bright colours, put on specially for the occasion.

"Miss," the block president began in a solemn tone of voice, "we hereby inform you that the tenants are not happy with your endeavours."

The girl looked at him quizzically, but all she could see was a blown up pufferfish. "What do you mean?"

"People are concerned."

"What about?"

"Why, about you, young lady! It's high time we were told who you might be, exactly. And what is it that you're doing here?"

She exhaled a sigh. "I'm ... I'm still trying to figure it out."

"And what, pray, gives you the right to disturb our peace of mind, and mess things up this way?"

Confused, she shrugged and shook her head. "How did I manage to do that?"

"You vandalized a perfectly fine patch of cabbage and planted an unnecessary row of flowers instead. Who does such a thing?"

"Flowers *and* salad greens," the girl offered, pointlessly again.

"Before you came, our cabbage garden used to the pride of all Chesternutville," a proud tenant joined in. "It was even awarded by the town council!"

"We won a shovel!" added with equal panache an invisible gardener.

"If I offended you, I apologize," the girl replied. "I didn't realise I was breaking a rule. There were plenty of cabbages and I thought it would be nice to plant something else among them, that's all."

"I think the flowers you planted are lovely." Though the old ballerina's voice came softly, those whispered words were a big brave step for a small sweet woman who had lived her entire life trying not to upset anybody.

"One row of flowers does not make summer!" came like a hammer the protest of a wise man.

"It's only a drop in the ocean!" pitched in an amateur angler with an interest in higher notions.

"Is cabbage not good enough for you, lassie?" inquired a woman with drawn-on thin black eyebrows that made her look constantly on the verge of a panic attack. "You consider yourself to be above cabbage – is that it?"

"Not at all. I do admit I wouldn't have cabbage every day. But that being said, my favourite food in the world is in fact a speciality my grandmother used to make when I was young: cabbage leaves stuffed with rice and minced meat. Come to think of it, perhaps that's one of the reasons why I came to visit_"

"You came here to steal our cabbages!" someone abruptly interrupted, not interested in extenuating circumstances or family relations.

"Cabbage thief!" a miffed shriek resounded.

The girl couldn't help but laugh out loud.

"She's laughing at us!"

"No, I'm not."

"I saw you the night you stole those cabbages!" shouted a sleepless old woman who couldn't see very well.

"I didn't steal. I picked them."

"Then why were you sneaking like a thief in the dark?" demanded to know a stark voice, its hair like yellow snow, with snake skin boots.

"I don't know. Maybe because I am a shy person. I don't like to be in the limelight."

The fashionista stifled a yawn, and a consequential man consequently asked:

"And then what did you do?"

Arms closed tight around her teddy bear, the old ballerina silently moved to stand by the girl.

"After I picked the cabbages?" the interrogated one replied, without really knowing why.

The crowd frowned a nod.

"I sold them at the market. And with the proceeds, I bought flowers and seeds which I planted the same day in the cabbage garden."

"And what did you do after that?"

"I went to have a shower and feed the cat."

"Cat? What cat!?" a duly outraged head exclaimed, ready to explode.

"You keep a cat in your flat!?" conscientiously stepped in the block president. "Have you declared it to the tenants' committee?"

"It's not my cat. It's just a cat that sometimes sleeps in my hat."

"What did she say?" asked an old dear who was deaf in one ear.

"Something about a cat wearing a hat. Or a hat that turned into a cat."

"She's contravening all rules of common sense!"

"She's obviously not one of ours!"

"She's a spy!"

"Or a traitor!"

At that moment, the girl understood. She was neither a foreigner, nor a stranger. She now recognised the submissive gene in herself. The accusations made against her were unfair, laughable and absurd, and yet she couldn't speak – couldn't utter a word. She simply bowed her head and quietly took the blame.

32

I TRAVEL LIGHT

When the crowd finally got bored of fighting someone who didn't fight back, and dispersed, the girl wrapped her arms around the brave old soul who had stood by her. "Thank you. I know how much strength and courage that took."

"I see myself in you, dear," the small ballerina said, slowly shaking her head. "The me I always wanted to be but never could." She wiped at her tears and laughed a shaky laugh. "Mind you, I don't even like baking pies! But I'm a lonely old woman and it's the only way I can get_"

Her voice broke again and the girl held her tighter. "I know."

"Are you still ... coming with me to the flea market?"

Yes, it was Sunday.

"Of course I am," the younger one nodded her head and smiled reassuringly.

They agreed to meet in a couple of hours, and then the girl returned to her flat only to realise, on opening her wardrobe, that she was wearing her last clean dress. Or well, to be exact, her last dress which used to be clean and was now crumpled and stained with dirt. Or mud.

Finding the laundry room locked, she went to the third floor to ask the block president for the key. To her surprise, it was the rich explorer who opened the door.

"I'm sorry… I was looking for the block president. Doesn't *he* live here?"

"We swapped flats yesterday," the explorer explained. "He was keen to move closer to the ground, so I just went along with it."

"I thought you've lived there for years."

"It's only a flat," the man smiled, inviting her in. "They are all pretty much the same, and it was no bother to just move a few stories up."

She nodded and looked around. Except for a rolled up sleeping bag, the living room was empty. "I won't hold you up any longer then. You must be busy unpacking."

"I'm already settled in," the explorer replied. "As you can see, I travel light."

They both smiled. "I do have a kettle though," he added, pointing to the kitchen. "And I make a mean cup of tea!"

The girl wanted to decline, but then reconsidered. Perhaps because she was curious, or maybe she just needed not to be alone right now. The cat sunbathing on the window sill gave her a knowing look, then lazily closed its eyes again.

"Is this *your* cat?" she laughed.

"I'd rather say I'm her pet," he retorted with a grin.

"Well, let me inform you that your cat is in the habit of sometimes taking a nap in my hat. And I do feed it every now and then. Hope you don't mind."

He gave a hearty laugh and shook his head. "Like owner, like pet. Both, wandering souls."

A moment of silence passed smoothly between them, as he was filling the kettle.

"Speaking of which_" The girl hesitated, not meaning to pry. "I was wondering ... why do you do it? What makes you travel the world?"

What are you looking for.

"Why wouldn't I? What's there to stop me?"

No, he wasn't going to answer that unspoken question.

33
REALITY BITES

Alex placed two sachets of pear and caramel tea, one in his tin cup and the other in the only glass he had available, then poured boiling water on top and added some milk.

"Sorry, I don't have any sugar."

"It's all right."

Handing her the cup, Alex took the glass, which he then quickly set back on the kitchen counter with a gasp. "Ouch, that was hot!"

They both laughed and she slowly took a sip, savouring the brew. Then she frowned, as if trying to retrace a memory.

Studying her from the corner of his eye, Alex decided she was an attractive woman. His age or probably younger. But he wasn't interested.

His lifestyle made him appealing to many women. And he'd heard all the questions before. That's why he now had the answers ready. Practiced answers, conveyed with due flippancy and poise.

People were curious and he couldn't always avoid their questions. However, what was truly in his heart, he kept to himself.

His wealth fascinated anyone who met him and that's why he'd stopped talking about it ages ago. Yes, he was rich. But contrary to common belief, he hadn't won the lottery. He'd won the money in a poker tournament. Not because he was a gambler, but because he could.

"Thank you for helping me ... in the garden."

"Don't mention it."

The woman seemed a bit disappointed. The truth is he'd enjoyed the gardening. It took his mind off other things. But he really didn't want to start a conversation.

"Have you ever been married?"

There it was. He should have seen it coming. To stall, Alex took a gulp of hot tea that scorched his throat all the way down to his guts. Swallowing a curse, he then stared hard at her, determined to promptly put a stop to any attempts of flirtation. But in her eyes, he saw no such thing. Only something that, for some strange reason, moved him. She reminded him of someone.

Finally, he nodded.

"And your wife ...?" she asked tentatively.

"What makes you think I only had one?" he grinned, but the next moment the grin faded under her earnest scrutiny. "My wife has long been my ex wife."

"Is that what you are trying to do? Escape? ..."

Alex gave a sharp laugh. She wasn't that far off the mark. Only that she was looking at it from the wrong angle. "My divorce didn't cause me any pain, if that's what you're asking. We simply grew apart and amicably decided to put an end to it."

"I'm sorry. I know it's none of my business. I just want to find some answers to my own questions, that's all."

Though he wasn't one to hear silent pleas, this time Alex heard it and answered. He told her about his travels, about how it had all started. By accident. When a mate, who was supposed to join an expedition to the desert, fell sick and Alex took his place. To break away from the heavy drinking and his other self-destructive habits. To forget. To fill the void.

Eventually, thanking him for the cup of tea, and above all for his eye-opening honesty, as she poetically put it, the woman stood up and started for the door, when suddenly she stopped in her tracks. "I was wondering ... could you possibly give me a hand with my bookkeeping? I am a freelance translator, you see. I know my words, but numbers terrify me."

"They terrify me too," he replied, looking a bit puzzled.

She frowned. "That's odd. I thought ... Aren't you an accountant?"

"Me, an accountant?" Alex almost choked with laughter. "Heavens, no! I'm a painter."

34
EVERYONE HAS A KEY

The girl slowly started down the stairs, deep in thought, pondering the twists and turns of the day, when someone came rushing up the steps, almost knocking her over. It was Bendis. Sobs racked her entire body. "I searched all over town and I can't_" Her voice broke. "I can't find it anywhere!"

"What is it? What did you lose?"

"My little ewe," Bendis whispered through her tears. "It's all I've got left. My heart and soul. It wanders off, but it always comes back. And now it's gone. Gone!"

Right then, answering some mysterious call, the lift stopped and opened its doors. Wiping her eyes, Bendis stepped inside and disappeared.

Returning to her flat with a heavy heart, the girl wasn't too surprised to find the huge cocoa box, the one filling her kitchen for the past few days, was finally gone. Without giving it a second thought, she grabbed her laundry basket, took the stairs to the ground floor, and knocked on a door.

The block president painstakingly slalomed through the piles of cardboard boxes, stacked up to the ceiling and filling almost every square inch of his new home. He opened the door with irritated look on his face. "Yes. How can I help you?"

"Hello." The girl wanted to apologize for her bad timing but then she changed her mind. "I need the key to the laundry room, please."

"Why is that?"

"I need to do my laundry." What more was there to be said?

"On a Sunday!?" he cried out, utterly appalled. "Nobody does laundry on Sundays. It's against the law."

"I'm sure whoever set that rule wouldn't want me to run out of clean clothes." It was a lie – a white one. She'd only run out of clean dresses.

"You've run out of clean clothes?" the block president gasped in disbelief. "How could you be so careless??"

It was none of his business, but the girl replied anyway. "It's simply gone out of my mind. May I have the key, please?"

"I don't know where it is," the block president replied gruffly before turning and shouting to the cardboard boxes: "Where is the key to the laundry room?"

"Everyone has their own key," came a similarly irate response from the other side of the pile.

"Well, I don't have one," retorted the girl from the second floor.

"She doesn't have one!" called back the block president. "Where did you put the bloody keys??"

"In one of these bloody boxes!!" his wife shot back.

"In which one??"

"I can't remember in which bloody box I put it! They are your keys, not mine! If you'd helped me pack, perhaps now you'd know where they are!"

The block president let out an exasperated sigh. "There's so much havoc and confusion whenever you're around," he groaned, turning back to face his unwelcome visitor, but the girl was gone.

35

AN ASTONISHING FIND

The flea market was bustling. People were selling all sorts, big and smalls, old toys, broken dreams, car parts, parts of their hearts, lamps and illusions that sparkled in the dark, accurate watches and clocks on which time had stopped, in a massively human attempt to clear their garages, their conscience, to cut their losses, to free their lofts and their memory of unwanted junk, to hear a kind word, maybe make a friend. There was real gold and fake troves. There were genuine works of art and cheap imitations, honest reproductions, pointless reiteration. They were selling little nothings and everything.

In her element, the old ballerina went treasure-hunting with a radiant smile on her face. Oblivious of her dress stained with dirt or mud, or both, the girl approached an antiquarian's stand and absent-mindedly picked up one of the old books on display. Its yellowed covers had seen better days. Opening the book randomly, at first the girl didn't realise what she saw. It was obviously a poem, judging by its form. Not printed, but written by hand. By two hands, alternating through the verse. On closer look, the girl froze. Her heart throbbing in her ears, she read the first stanza. Slowly, having to repeat under breath every word, her brain suddenly hazed in a thick cotton-like mist.

> It's a fortuity of my being:
> And then, the happiness in this heart of mine
> Is stronger than me, stronger than my bones,
> That you crush in your embrace –
> Ever so painful, ever so divine.

The girl swallowed hard. It was *her* handwriting. And the words sounded strangely familiar. She read on.

> Let's talk, let's speak, let's utter words,
> Long and glassy, like chisels that separate
> The cold river from the delta's hot curves,
> Day from night, slate from slate.

Beyond any doubt, this was… Lavender Boy's handwriting. And the last two stanzas were written again in their alternating two hands.

Happiness, take me on high and slam
My brow against the moon,
Until my world, overlong and in excess,
May turn into a column or something
Much higher, something soon.

It's so good that you are, so wondrous that I am!
Two different songs, colliding, intertwining,
Two colours that never met before,
One from down below, turned toward the ground,
The other from high above, almost torn
In this unseen before fiery storm
Of the wonder that you are, and the fortuity that I am.

She gasped. This was *the* poem. The one she wanted to translate some day. For him. For Lavender Boy. But apparently it had been already translated … long before. And obviously they both must have known the translation, because the handwriting was definitely theirs.

But how was that possible? The two of them hadn't really known each other for that long. They'd never even met face to face. And yet, the poem translated with the words which only existed in her head, was there, black on white, written down by Lavender Boy and herself.

What was this? What was going on?

36
IN AND OUT OF THE WOODS

"How much for the book?"

It was peanuts. It made sense.

After they returned from the flea market, remembering the little sheep she saw in town yesterday, the girl went straight to the top floor and knocked on Bendis' door. There was no answer. *Maybe it's better this way*, the girl thought. What was the point in telling someone you saw something they held dear only to let it slip through your fingers?

The moment she returned to her flat and closed the door behind her, the doorbell rang. It was the postman.

"Working even Sundays? I do admire your diligence," she had to admit, despite everything.

"When duty calls ..."

After they both sat down at the kitchen table, the postman looked around and commented with a smile: "The box of cocoa is finally gone. I'm glad."

"It's good you're here. I have an urgent letter to send." Hurriedly, the girl emptied her pockets and set their contents on the table. The crumpled napkin, the clover-shaped 'Little March', the message that reminded her she wasn't alone, and the list of things she'd been randomly jotting down on a piece of paper, trying to remember. She didn't need the last one anymore, so she turned the sheet over and quickly copied on the back the translated poem she found in the book.

DO YOU KNOW THIS POEM? she wrote below the translation. HAVE YOU EVER WRITTEN IT DOWN WITH YOUR VERY HAND?

She placed the Little March in the centre of the page, then folded the letter and handed it to the postman. "It's for_"

"I know. Lavender Boy."

After the postman left, the girl took the book she'd bought at the flea market and slowly opened it. Again, her and Lavender Boy's handwriting, this time colliding, intertwining in each sentence. The title on the page read *In And Out Of the Woods*.

The wood. She swallowed hard. It couldn't be. Still, she read on. It was all there. How on an ordinary day, one that could never bring back the normalcy of yesterday, she went out for a walk and never came back.

'In the quiet dark,' she remembered out loud, 'all masks will fall and break to pieces, and you will forget everything. Your name, the shape of your heart, the way you used to love, and think, and be proud when things were normal.'

It was true. The words reminded her of how she had felt so utterly broken, and painfully new, and the childlike defencelessness that came with it. How grateful she'd become for a smile, how easy to make her cry.

'You won't even dare to look at yourself in the mirror for fear you'll see a total stranger staring back.'

She read, and reading, she understood: she wasn't lost in that wood – she had been hiding there. Because it felt safer than anything else. A warm, nurturing place like a mother's embrace.

'It hurts', she whispered the written words, 'to stand in a crowd where everybody else has their shields, their swords and their sun glasses on, and all you're wearing is your bare soul and a broken heart.'

The next line filled her eyes and the words turned into tears.

'This is a map to help you find your way out.'

Out, she repeated under her breath. Out, but never back.

'All you have to do' – a lump rose in her throat – 'is breathe in, and breathe out.' She did exactly that, because she needed to. 'Day in, day out – breathe in, breathe out. Day after day, take one small step after the other. And when you've walked several circles, and are no longer afraid to look yourself in the eyes and see one and all, you will find the door you've been searching for. A secret code only you can decipher. A miracle only you can achieve.'

37

BY SOME MIRACLE

A sudden knock on the door made her start and look up. She set the book aside, wiped her tears and went to answer, hoping that, by some miracle, it would be the postman returning with a letter from Lavender Boy. But it was the explorer. No, the painter.

"About what you asked before," he began, "it's just occurred to me that ..."

"Will you please come inside?"

He nodded and followed her into the kitchen, smiling at the amount of books scattered all around.

"Thank you." Her back turned to him so he couldn't see her tears, she set to make two cups of instant coffee. "Thank you for telling me your story." The water came to a boil, almost spilling out of the kettle. "It's the kindest gift you can give to a stranger." She poured the hot water over the coffee powder and the brews frothed up. "Because you opened up your heart, I somehow feel less lonely. Less out of place." She stirred the coffee and set the two cups on the table.

"By the way," – he extended his arm out, "I'm Alex."

Breathing out a sigh, she closed her eyes tight.

"I am_"

It must have been her accent, or maybe Alex was simply absent-minded, because he just shook her hand with a broad smile on his face. "Nice to meet you, M."

As they were drinking their coffee, she told Alex her story, or at least as much as she could remember. She told him about her world of words and languages that constantly merged and emerged, about being lost in the dark wood, about the strange dreams she'd been having lately, about her soulmate who was out there, but she didn't know how to reach. About it all being so hopeless and senseless.

"I had a strange dream too," Alex returned. "Not so long ago. During the bank holiday week. I dreamt of a man who asked me to paint something on the Great Wall. For someone to see."

She raised an eyebrow. "How intriguing."

"What's really funny is that I actually ... did it," Alex laughed. "I actually painted the scene on the wall. Almost got caught by the police!"

"Wow! she returned with a chuckle. "What on earth made you do that?"

"The bloke in my dream – he sounded so urgent. You know, as if someone's life depended on it. Anyway," – Alex downed the contents of his cup and stood up, "time to go. Thank you for the coffee." In front of the door he paused, then his eyebrows shot up. "Blimey, I almost forgot what I came to tell you! If you need some help with your bookkeeping, why not ask Marta?"

"Marta? Who is Marta?"

"My next door neighbour. I thought you were friends. She's the little old lady who bakes those great pies."

"You mean ... the ballerina?"

Alex gave a good-hearted laugh, stepping out into the landing. "I don't think she's ever been an actual ballerina. But I'm pretty sure she used to be a bookkeeper." With a wink, he started up the stairs.

"What was the scene you painted?" she called after him.

"The one that bloke asked for in my dream?"

She nodded.

"A lavender field." And with that, Alex disappeared up the steps, leaving her wide-eyed and speechless.

38
SNOW IN JUNE

It wasn't Lavender Boy who had painted the lavender field on the great grey wall. It was Alex.

Suddenly, huge heavy snowflakes began falling from the sky, floating weightless in the air, filling it entirely, before they'd touch the ground and die. It was snowing in June.

The girl thought it must have been her. She didn't know those were the tears of Bendis, the goddess living on the top floor. The goddess of the forests, eternal love and the moon, whom her people had turned into a disenchanted strawberry picker. Bendis was crying out her sorrow, and her tears froze into snowflakes and were falling painfully, enveloping the world. Snow in June. Shocking, and heartbreakingly beautiful.

Then the doorbell rang. It was the postman with a much needed answer.

Hands trembling, the girl unfolded the letter and something fell from inside the paper, making a slight clanking noise on the naked floor. She carefully picked up the small object. It was a clover-shaped lucky charm. The Little March she ... Why did he send it back?

She stared at the letter and read as if in a dream.

The poem is one you translated for me long ago. Together, we wrote it down in our story so we would never forget. Together, we drew a map to always find our way back.

I am right here, my love, I never left. And for as long as there shall be light in this soul of mine, I will love you and I will wait.

I am standing in the crowd, watching people go past, and every now and then I talk to strangers as if they were my friends. I tell them about you, and I ask them to give you my love if your paths ever cross. With their help, I send you pieces of my heart to remind you there is nothing that can ever break us apart.

Once I met a painter and asked him to paint a lavender field on a wall, for you to see and remember me.

Then on another day, I met a woman who came from the land of your people and I asked her to give you this Little March that you once gave me. To keep you safe and show you the way.

I am right here, my love, I never left. And for as long as there shall be light in this soul of mine, I will love you and I will wait.

Silent tears rolling down her face, she turned around, to thank the postman. But he was gone.

39
GIBBERISH

The girl opened the front door and stepped outside. The landing was empty. Her gaze slowly drifting over the corridor, something caught her attention. She looked again, this time deliberately, at the numbers of the three flats, including her own, that filled the second floor. From left to right, they read 8, 1 and 6. Strange numbering system.

Intrigued, the girl slowly walked upstairs only to find the next storey presented the same oddity and randomness. Here, from left to right, the flats were numbered 3, 5 and 7. Repeating the numbers under her breath, something felt mysteriously familiar. As if she'd seen the same pattern before. Sensing the rustling of paper, she reached into her pocket and took out the crumpled napkin she'd meant to get rid of. In the middle of the napkin was the gibberish scribbled by the ruddy-faced old man she met at the pub, and in a corner something had made her draw a square the other day, while waiting for the traffic lights to turn green.

4		2
3	5	7
8	1	6

Glancing at the numbers written in the square, her breath caught. *The answer is always nine,* she remembered the words that unveiled what the blank concealed.

On the top floor, it came as no surprise to her that the numbers read, from left to right: 4, 9 and 2.

Returning to her flat, she took a pen and filled in the blank.

4	**9**	2
3	5	7
8	1	6

The moment she wrote *9* in the central upper square, the gibberish in the middle of the napkin turned into an intelligible message:

To love another, you must first learn to love yourself.
To love yourself, you must first know who you are.

The very last line remained blurred, and the sound of the doorbell broke the spell of the moment.

She opened the door, expecting to see the postman. Instead, it was a young police officer who smiled sheepishly back at her.

"Miss, complaints have been made against you," he began in a boyishly solemn tone of voice. "Some tenants claim you might be a ..." – sharp cough, blushing with embarrassment – "spy or a traitor. Therefore," he shrugged apologetically, "I am arresting you on suspicion of strange and disruptive behaviour. You don't have to say anything, but what you say may be put into writing and given in evidence."

40
FREEDOM

The occupants of the other cells at the Chesternutville police station had all been locked up for minor offences. Who for shoplifting, who for dreaming out loud; who for lending their body, who for selling their soul; who for aimless driving, who for sailing against mainstream; who for drunken elation, who for knocking down a door.

A man who'd been arrested for walking with his head in the clouds started whistling the tune to a song he didn't know the words of. The female thief occupying the next cell knew the lyrics, but she couldn't speak his language very well.

The sound of the sung poem stirred something in the girl's heart. She recognised it as part of her heritage, a mysterious language she understood but had forgotten to speak. Weary of prose and longing for poetry, the translator therefore happily set off to translate the lyrics for the repeat daydreamer.

She didn't translate just the words. She translated their music, their bittersweet flavour, their light, their shadowy swords, the secret sound that, unseen, touches deep, hidden chords. She translated what was said and, wordlessly, what was left untold.

It was a beautiful song she'd never heard before. One about waiting the long wait. Sitting in pubs with only Time for a mate, drinking for joy and then to forget, while waiting for the one who would make the wait worthwhile. Every now and then, a star would flash bright in the dark of your night, only to turn into a swallow by daylight. Again and again, all you seem to find in your weary sky are swallow-stars which shine briefly and then die – or fly off to find another sky. And you keep waiting, with only Time for a mate, sitting in pubs, drinking for joy and then to forget – waiting for the one who might never come.

When the drunken dreamer heard what the song was about, he laughed out loud. And then he fell to his knees and wept.

The girl didn't know exactly why, but the lyrics made her think about the ruddy-faced old man she had met at the pub.

After that, word got around and the requests came flowing. Each prisoner had a favourite song they loved listening to, without knowing what was actually being sung. The most hardened offenders were secretly attached to cartoon tunes which reminded them of their childhood and bluer skies. And the translator obliged, taking them to realms of eternal sunshine where rainbows painted everything in the colours of love.

For others, who felt displaced and estranged, foreigners everywhere, even in their own land, the lyrics she translated smelled of violets and the green grass of home, and made her sense the call of her own roots. Some wanted to escape through her words to secret make-believe worlds. A few needed to be reminded of true love, and of the truth which lay hidden in each human heart.

Some yearned for the smoothness of fairy tales, others for the harshness of reality. Fairy tales were simple and made sense; reality was convoluted and absurd. The words of the first were heartbreakingly gentle, they hardly made a sound; the others were a discrepant, deafening shout.

And yet, in a mysterious way, each song matched the soul who'd requested it, and all the songs told of the same thing. The immense beauty of being.

And the girl translated one song after the other, remembering all the languages she knew, moulding them together till all the words turned into music and filled her entirely. For the first time she truly saw the creator in the translator – there were clues sprinkled along the way like star dust she could taste on her lips, in her mouth, to the core of her heart.

Some of those clues she found hidden in the title of a childish song, made up of three mundane looking words which contained two matching sets of numbers, an ancient sound and other words, an unseen infinity symbol, a perfect circle, mirrors within and without, and telling sums she recognised. A sublime touch of the untranslatable, which was more or less what the song was about.

Mysteries were revealed at every step, gradually releasing the top, middle and base notes of a heavenly perfume, until her joy, spilling out fragrant and bright, pervaded the air, touching all the lost souls, in each and every cell. And even though her body was trapped in a certain way, never before had the translator's heart felt more open and free.

41

THE INTERVIEW

Getting word of the stranger who was thought to be a spy or a traitor, the local newspaper sent out a reporter to interview the suspect detained at the police station.

"Will you please tell us a little bit about yourself," the journalist prodded with practiced good-naturedness.

"That's why I came here," the girl confessed. "To find out who I am."

Sensing the slippery terrain of spirituality, the female reporter quickly steered the conversation onto earthlier waters. She didn't need Hamlet – Hamlet didn't sell newspapers. "What is it that you do for a living?"

"I translate books. Mainly fiction."

To keep the conversation going and put her interlocutor at ease, the reporter resorted to a ruse she was sure would please: "What is it like? To translate a story, I mean."

The girl grew thoughtful for a few moments.

"No two stories are ever the same. Every translation is a new beginning. At first, it feels like ... I don't know

– walking into a crowd. Everything is new, everything is foreign and loud. I immerse myself into the unknown, and I am a painter. I brush the commotion, I grab the colours that first meet the eye, I clear, I lighten, I sharpen, I dry.

"And I keep walking, and become an explorer. I travel though space and time, myths and mysteries, I search probable facts, discover histories written and rewritten, unbury what is possibly true and what isn't told, I see life erupting and lives put on hold, I uncover one cipher after the other, find clues sprinkled along the way, rediscover thoughts and ideas, I recognise what's rightly said, what's misconstrued, and what sounds odd, I recognise feelings, emotions, I explore shades, nuances, possibilities and improbabilities, heights and depths, highs and lows. I travel all over the world only to know I'm nowhere a stranger.

"And when I reach the deepest of heights, when I'm on top of the word, I feel like a goddess. Under my eyes, empires rise and fall, histories live and die. I see the circles in the sand. It's always the same, again and again, a never-ending game.

"And the goddess turns into a ballerina dancing weightlessly through worlds of words. Worlds that belong to others, while being all mine.

"And after all is said and done, at the end of the day, when all music is gone, I become a night street sweeper. I unclutter, I clean, I see lovers kissing under the moon, I hear the lonely cry in the dark, I scoop up the pieces of broken dreams, pick up a broken heart, I taste the bitter sweetness of small victories and great defeat. After the party is over, at night, when matters are settled and souls go to sleep, I turn off the lights and sweep the streets so that a new day may begin."

With a triumphant grin, the journalist surreptitiously made a note: The subject is deranged. And poetic.

The translator looked her in the eye and exhaled a resilient sigh. "It's an unglorified, painstakingly strenuous and yet important job. One which, apart from skill, requires a tremendous amount of dedication and selflessness. Like carrying someone else's child."

To fill the remaining time assigned for the interview, the reporter asked her a few more questions.

Inconsequential fillers, really. She already had all the material she needed.

After the journalist left, alone in her cell, the girl started to check her pockets, but quickly realised the napkin had been confiscated by the custody sergeant when they brought her here, along with the other road signs and clues she had written down. It didn't matter. She already knew them all by heart.

And the girl also knew that what the napkin said was only part of the message. She reached deep within and remembering, recited the words out loud:

Knowledge is power, but knowledge without wisdom is joyless nothingness.

And the words materialized on the wall of her cell. Then something Bendis had said sounded clearly in her memory, merging with something else that continued with the first line the napkin had revealed. And as she was thinking it, everything was being written on the wall, word after word, line after line.

Wisdom is only achieved when your heart meets the heart of things.

And when all wisdom is gone, all we have left to fight off the darkness is love.

To love another, you must first learn to love yourself.

Taking a deep breath, the girl uttered the words that came before the last line – the one she hadn't been able to read because the letters on the napkin were blurred.

To love yourself, you must first know who you are.

No sooner had the words appeared on the wall when the mysterious last line followed, revealing itself, loud and clear, right before her eyes.

You are me, and we are ready.

42

UNEXPECTED RESCUE

On Monday morning, the local newspaper printed an article that had the entire town talking. The headline, overwhelming the front page in flamboyant bold letters, read: ***Translator Accused Of Being A Spy Or A Traitor Lends Herself As Surrogate Mother.*** Posted on the world wide web, the scoop went viral.

At the bottom of the page, another article announced, in a more sedate tone and manner, that the Chesternutville yearly festival would begin tomorrow, around lunchtime, with the mayor's speech and the drawing competition.

That day Alex did something he rarely used to do: he bought the newspaper. Skipping over the flashy article that filled the front page and reading the one at the bottom instead, he then went to get a box of coloured chalk and register in the drawing contest.

M. needed a door. And he was going to draw one for her on the Great Grey Wall.

The following day, the charges made against the girl from Lavender Street were dropped and she was set free. How come, she never found out. She simply put it down to the lucky charm attached to the front of her dress – the clover-shaped Little March now blended into the pattern of the fabric, right across her heart.

In truth, the reason behind her release couldn't have been more fortuitous. In fact, it was of an official, convoluted and fashion-related nature, and accordingly prosaic. As it happens, on reading the newspaper article, the mayor's wife – who for the last couple of days, unbeknownst to the girl, had been advocating *The Dressmaker's Encyclopaedia* as an essential read for the citizens of Chesternutville – put two and two together and realised that the prisoner suspected to be a spy or a traitor was the very translator of the book she was championing, in a cunningly home-tailored attempt to wash the infamous unicorn matter out of the Chesternutters' minds. Hence, after a short and some might say heated conversation with her husband, the town's first lady and the mayor quickly agreed that a new scandal, and especially one which would personally involve the two of them, was the last thing Chesternutville needed. And that's, in a nutshell, how the charges against the obscure translator promptly disappeared as if they had never existed, without further ado, delay or consequences.

The custody officer retrieved the girl's property – the two sheets of paper and the napkin on which all they'd found written was gibberish – and tried to hand it over to her.

She shook her head and smiled. "It's all right. I don't need them anymore."

43

POINTLESS

The girl walked out of the police station and raised her eyes towards the dull sun. She was ready.

Suddenly, she spotted the little sheep that had caused havoc in the traffic the other day. The small animal now had a lead balloon tied by a long red string around its neck and was struggling to drag the burdensome weight, while two heavy-set men that looked like council workers were pulling it roughly by a leash.

The girl started to say something, but then stopped herself. She knew it would be pointless. Was this the submissive gene keeping her quiet again? She lifted her gaze back towards the washed out, lifeless sky. No, this was a gene that ran much deeper; the gene that knew.

Oblivious of the man who was drawing a door for her on the Great Grey Wall, the girl started in the opposite direction. She needed to get back to her flat, and then home.

The mayor stepped onto the podium and looked around. It was only 10 a.m. and except for a couple of street sweepers, his ever-present entourage and the occasional passer-by, the central square was deserted. It didn't matter, really.

The town festival had been announced to officially open around noon, and the mayor was a man of his word. It's just that he had other plans for lunch. Anyways, the scene was set – a large flock of cardboard sheep, with three actors dressed as shepherds in the middle – and the television cameras were at the ready.

In the distance, a man was feverishly drawing something on the Great Grey Wall. Something rectangular, that looked like a door. Since the competition hadn't officially started, without giving it a second thought, the mayor decided the early drawer would be by all means disqualified.

Then the town leader cleared his voice, gave a subtle nod to the television crews and smiled a cordial, politically correct smile into the cameras.

44
THE WRATH OF THE GODDESS

By the time the mayor finished his speech, declaring the festivities officially opened and the lonely drawer officially disqualified, the central square was already filled with an audience of active participants – citizens who considered it their duty to always comply and be there, no matter why, no matter when, no matter where.

After a round of applause and cheers, they all put on a duly grave face for the town's anthem – a strange and mysterious ancient song none of them knew the meaning of, that had travelled by word of mouth over thousands of years, ever changing shape and form, turning from chant into carol and eventually ballad, about two shepherds who plotted to murder a third one. What all the extant versions had in common was the fact that, while knowing he was going to be killed, the sacrificial shepherd accepted it as his fate and took no action. His only wish was that, after his death, he'd be left on the hillside, under the open sky, surrounded by his flock.

In the latest version of the song, that had been adopted as the town's anthem, a local poet had added a twist to the story, introducing a little ewe that, on warning the shepherd about the evil plan of the other two, he entrusted with telling the rest of his flock that he simply went away to marry a beautiful princess, the bride of the world.

While eager spectators were solemnly humming the lyrics they didn't understand, staring pensively at the symbolic flock of fake sheep and curiously eyeing the three rental shepherds, the mayor gave a discrete nod to one of the council workers, signalling him to proceed with the plan. It was going to be the cherry on the cake, this. The bloody cherry on the cake!

The following moment, glad to obey his boss' command and to the public's utter delight, the council worker appeared from behind the podium, pulling by the leash a little sheep that physically struggled to carry the metaphorical weight of its bestowed secret, materialized in the form of a lead balloon. People made way for the living allegory, enthusiastically clapping their hands when suddenly the cloudless sky turned black and an inhuman scream pierced the air.

Everybody froze. The earth trembled, the mountains shook and the seas roared. With burning coals blazing in her eyes, Bendis soared above on the wings of the wind, parting the dark skies, then swooped fiercely into the middle of the crowd. Mad and larger than life, she was shining a blinding light, terrifying the mortals around her to death.

"You awful, awful people!" her voice resounded like a thunder. "How many times did you fall on your knees, hurting and broken, in my woods, among my trees, under my moon?" Darkening, she slowly looked around, encompassing the whole crowd. "And how many times did I lift you up, heal your wounds, take you to my pastures, let you drink from my springs of cool water?" All those Bendis stared in the eye, turned into stone. At a second glance, the stone shattered to pieces. "You always ask, and I always give, and you always take. You take it all and let it slip though your wasteful fingers and you never give anything back. And now you're even trying to take my heart and soul!"

Tears streaming down her face, the goddess went to the little ewe that was crying too, and gently removing the leash and breaking the string tied to the lead balloon, lifted the small animal in her arms and cradled it against her chest.

45

A LOVE SONG

Alex had just finished drawing the door on the wall when suddenly the day turned into night and he heard an inhuman, heartbreaking cry.

Though they lived in the same building, Alex and Bendis had never met before. They were both private, didn't send postcards to neighbours, didn't let everybody know what they ate, what they drank, how they felt every single moment of every single day. In a world where everybody had something to talk about, those who had something to say kept quiet.

That's why when Alex turned around and looked towards the central square, he didn't see his neighbour from the fourth floor. All he saw ... was – he let out a gasp. All he saw was a girl amid a sea of stone. A being of immense beauty, her dark hair a forest that flowed, a shimmering stream, its waves enveloping her like folded broken dreams, all the way to the ground. She was crying without making a sound. And yet, he recognised her silent voice. It was a voice he knew well.

In what felt like the blink of an eye, he was right there, before the breathtakingly beautiful angel that fate had somehow marooned on this improbable island of his existence. It was her – he exhaled deeply, as if he'd been holding his breath forever. It was her, no doubt – his dream girl. The one he longed for every night, and every day. The one he spent a lifetime looking for. But he only ever found her in his dreams. There, they talked, they uttered words, long and glassy, they opened their wings and flew, they laughed, they cried, they loved, they made love, they touched the sky. He was the cold river running through the delta's hot curves. She was a skylark and he was a falcon; two different songs colliding, intertwining. And every day, and every night, they were two colours that had never met before. One from down below, turned toward the ground, the other from high above, almost torn.

He reached out, gently brushed a curl away from her temple and cupped her face in the palm of his hand. The girl didn't pull away. She just looked at him and smiled through her tears. "It's you."

"I carried you in my dreams all my life. I dreamt you were a royal scribe's daughter."

"And you were the painter who worked with my father," said the one who once used to be known as Ninsar.

He smiled back. "Your father had named you after a goddess."

"They call me Bendis now."

"You'll always be a goddess to me, no matter what people call you."

Overlong suppressed tears filled her eyes again, and she put the little ewe back down on the ground.

He kissed her hair, her eyes, her lips. "I crossed the driest deserts, climbed the highest mountains, sailed the deepest seas, looking for you."

"I lived a thousand lifetimes waiting."

"Remember this?" He took a small clay tablet out of his breast pocket and handed it to her. "I carry it with me everywhere I go. On all my travels – as a talisman."

The words were written in an ancient script, but she recognised her own handwriting. The message read:

Your goodness and love will follow me for as long as I shall breathe, and you will dwell in my heart forever.

"It's a love poem I once sang for you."

"I found it by accident, in a faraway land," Alex replied. "You must have left it there to remind me of you." He crushed her in a desperate, heavenly painful embrace. "And it broke my heart to think you were somewhere out there, feeling lonely and forgotten, when you were never alone. And I never forgot."

46
THE VEIL IS LIFTED

In the meantime, little knowing what was happening in the central square, as soon as the translator from Lavender Street got back to her flat on the second floor, she lay down on the couch and fell into a deep sleep. When she woke up, a red sun, as if set on fire by the illustrator of a children's book, was already descending beyond the mountains to drown in the sea.

The girl took her muddy dress off, had a shower, then stepped naked in front of the mirror and looked at herself. It was the first time in a long while she felt strong enough to do that. *I've changed and thought you might not recognise the person I now happened to be.* She looked herself in the eyes, noticing the lines, drawn in the corners by laughter, or tears, or time, then her face relaxed into a smile. There was nothing wrong with what she saw. The reflection was not scary or staring, it was smiling back at her. Everything was fine. Everything was as it was supposed to be.

She had to walk these circles, in order, to get here.

Opening her wardrobe, the girl remembered she'd run out of clean dresses. *For the last few weeks,* she laughed and cried at the same time, *I put on a nice dress every day, in the hope we might somehow meet, run by chance into each other on the street, or that you might perhaps see me from a distance, from somewhere near or far. In case you had forgotten my face, I wanted you to like what you saw, to think that I looked nice, like someone you could maybe love.*

She put on a clean old T-shirt and a pair of jeans, and wiped off her tears. *But if it is you, I know you will be able to see underneath, behind and beyond no matter what may be. And you will know this is me.*

The smile returned, along with the certainty, and stayed.

And for as long as there shall be you and I, our love will never die. It will live on, in no matter what shape or form.

Moving to stand by the window, she gazed at the painted-on dusk engulfing the land, and thought about the little sheep being pulled on a leash while dragging that heavy lead balloon. Ever since she saw it, she couldn't get the image out of her mind. It had even pervaded her sleep. And then there was the mystery of Lavender Street. But that wasn't a mystery anymore. What's in a name, after all?

The sound of the doorbell put an end to her thoughts, a fresh start. It was Bendis and Alex.

"We are getting married!" they beamed, their arms laced, their soul made whole. "Come on, let's celebrate!"

The girl stared at them, but all she could see was Romeo and Juliet, resurrected by some miracle and finally becoming all they were meant to be.

47
ON TOP OF THE WORLD

The girl stuck a pen and a blank sheet of paper in her pocket, then went to get Marta and they joined Alex and Bendis on the rooftop.

Larger than life, the moon, that seemed to have become one with the sun, hung low, setting the whole garden aglow. At first there was one shooting star, after which came shyly another, a third travelled from afar and burst with joy, like fireworks, right above the crowned heads of the hosts, and then all the other stars, giddy and silvery gold, let themselves fall from the sky in an unseen before shower of sparkling light, settling bright on every branch of every tree, on every blade of grass, in the bride's hair, in the groom's eyes.

The mountains and the sea performed the wedding ceremony.

Then the groom played the saxophone, accompanied by an orchestra of singing birds from all over the world and the wind rustling through the trees, a jazzy melody, his gaze never leaving the eyes of the one he'd spent an eternity looking for.

Dizzy with glee, Marta jumped up and danced, gracefully looping turns and pliés, grands jetés and pirouettes as wide as fully open wings.

When the groom stopped playing and embraced his bride, all the flowers around released their colours into the wide open air, where they floated and danced like weightless balloons, higher and higher into the sky, releasing their fragrance that turned into music, and the music fell back towards the ground like a cool summer rain on a hot sunny night, embracing the universe.

And they partied all night.

Eventually, Marta was the first one to excuse herself and leave, exhausted and exhilarated at the same time.

The translator was tired too, but ready. Watching the bride and groom dance in each other's arms under the whole of the moon, she saw how they gradually turned, from a middle-aged A and a middle-aged B, into a breathtakingly beautiful boy and girl, their love ever young, and perfect, and free. Beside them, the ewe-lamb floated contentedly in the air, light as a feather.

Before daybreak, taking the lamb into her arms, Bendis waved good-bye, and then the bride and groom opened their wings and away they flew into the sky.

48
HOME

The moment Alex and Bendis disappeared into the sky, everything around vanished as if it had never existed; the rooftop garden, the cabbage garden, the block of flats, Lavender Street, the whole town.

The girl was standing again with her feet on the ground, and there was nothing around. Not a single thing, not a single sound.

She slowly breathed in, then slowly breathed out and closed her eyes.

When she opened them again, she saw the postman standing next to her.

"Long time no see," he smiled, lighting a cigar.

"You never told me you were a smoker," she commented, somewhat surprised.

"You never asked." He turned to face the girl and looked deeply into her eyes. "So tell me, have you figured it out yet?"

"I think so."

"And did you manage to understand what this was? Is Chesternutville the land of your people?"

The girl laughed and shook her head. "I carry my roots in my heart."

"How about the languages you speak?" he said.

"They've all merged into one."

"Do you know what you have to do now?"

"I hope so," she smiled.

"Are you ready?"

When she nodded her head, he vanished.

Her heart started fluttering, and then the flutter turned into pounding. *Breathe in, breathe out.* She looked around one more time, the nothingness making her shudder. I *am* ready. Taking the pen and paper from her pocket, she wrote down the simplest words:

I WANT TO LIVE

And as soon as she finished writing, a dazzling light surrounded her then faded slowly; the steady beep of a monitor and the mystery of a joyful face. She was where she'd always been.

She closed her eyes and saw the wood again, but no longer was it dark. Alongside, ran a long country road leading to hidden paths, mysteries, treasures, playful words, songs and the gift of life.

And on the right, in the green, wide open field? There we were. You and me, walking hand in hand among daffodils and other wild things.

She squeezed the fingers that held hers and smiled.

EPILOGUE

Thousands of years later, some of the words the old scribe wrote saved his great-great-granddaughter's soul.

Chesternutville continued to exist right there, between heaven and hell, just off the coast of reality, in someone else's dreams or maybe somewhere else.

The flower calendar was a huge success. It sold in greater numbers than the publisher's bestselling book of all times. The young editor was promoted and became one of the most highly esteemed book editors in town. He could see in the heart of things and knew daffodils belonged to ever flowing springs.

The block president on the other hand, was less fortunate. His wife ran off with the car mechanic from Flat no. 12. In her stead, the explorer's cat came to delve into the block president's head.

As for the darkness Bendis' sorrow had brought upon the land, when it lifted, the people in the central square awoke as from a long sleep, and saw the light of dawn. Their hearts of stone had been shattered and turned into hearts of flesh, beating to a secret sound. Hearing the call of distant drums, some found the door Alex had drawn on the Great Grey Wall, and left.

For some, it was too late. They were too old, too tired, there was too much or too little to be said.

Not long after she met the girl who had briefly sojourned on the second floor, Marta died and according to her wish, she was buried with her teddy bear. She died happy. After a lifetime of keeping her head bowed, she had lifted her eyes and lived. Some remembered her fondly for her many a scrumptious cake and pie. But only a few ever knew that once, on top of the world, under the sunny moon, she had opened her wings and let her soul fly, free as a bird, in the open sky.

That winter, the row of flowers died back to the ground. The annuals didn't make a comeback the following spring, but the rain washed the seeds away and forever filled the town, beyond and above, painting everything in the colours of love.

AFTERWORD

As for the mysterious childish song which had proved to be so revealing to the translator when she was locked in her cell at the Chesternutville police station, one of the main things that had caught her attention was a mirrored sequence contained by the second word of the song's title, namely the letters *ab ba* which, in the ancient script, to her wide open eyes, read as 96 69 – an unseen infinity and perfect circle.

The song was called the **cabba**ge garden.

With Gratitude to…

The English language, all its great voices, and my Romanian heritage – together you've made this story take shape and come to life.

My husband and best friend – for believing in me and acting as my editor on this manuscript. I love you, Paul.

The Romanian poet Nichita Stănescu – for having written the original poem I've translated and slightly adapted under the title *It's A Fortuity of My Being*, the words of which run as a red thread throughout my narrative;

Arthur Benjamin and Michael Shermer – for their book, *Secrets of Mental Math: The Mathemagician's Guide to Lightning Calculation and Amazing Math Tricks*, which contains the maths trick and the magic square featured in *The Cabbage Garden*;

Maria Uca Marinescu, a Romanian explorer and a formidable woman I greatly admire. One of her conversations with a journalist was the inspiration for Alex's answers in Ch. 20;

The Hungarian band Kispál és a Borz. Their song, *Csillag vagy fecske,* is the base for the girl's first translation after she is locked up – the song about swallow-stars and waiting the long wait. Just like the translator in the story, I have a peculiar and deep relationship with the original language of the lyrics (albeit that the language referred to in the book is a different one). Hungarian is part of my heritage. I inherited it through my maternal grandmother, and that's why it is so dear to my heart. What's peculiar is that, while I can understand every word, Hungarian is, unfortunately, a language I've forgotten to speak. But it's never too late to remember,

Bendis, the Dacian goddess of the Moon, love, and the forests;

My Mother, whose embrace has always cast away the darkness;

The little ewe-sheep – one of the four fundamental myths of Romanian literature;

And most importantly, *you* – for having taken the time to read my story.

Needless to say, Chesternutville is not Romania, or any other given country. It simply lies off the shore of consciousness not far from beyond. But you know that by now?

Printed in Great Britain
by Amazon